# SEARCH

# PARTY

For more information, write to:
Permissions
Inlandia Institute
4178 Chestnut Street Riverside, CA 92501

Published in 2025 by Inlandia Books
inlandiainstitute.org

Cover design and layout by JeremyJohnParker.com
ISBN: 978-1-955969-40-6
eISBN: 978-1-955969-41-3

Library of Congress Control Number: 2025934656

This is a work of fiction. Names, characters, places and incidents either are products of the author's imagination or are used fictitiously. Any resemblance to actual events or locales or persons, living or dead, is entirely coincidental.

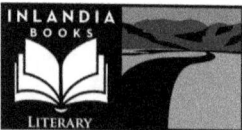

Printed and bound in the United States Distributed by Ingram
Published by Inlandia Institute
Riverside, California
www.InlandiaInstitute.org
First Edition

# SEARCH

A Novel

# PARTY

## RENÉ SOLIVAN

AN INLANDIA INSTITUTE PUBLICATION

RIVERSIDE, CALIFORNIA

# PREFACE

The unexpected passing of René Solivan came as a profound loss to those who knew and loved him. As a son, brother, uncle, cousin, and friend, René had a singular way of connecting with people through his humor, his sharp insights, and his deep reserve of empathy. His death left an unfillable void, but it also revealed the many gifts he left behind, not the least of which is the manuscript for *Search Party*, a deeply personal and stunningly crafted work that captures so much of his essence.

In discovering this unpublished novel, which he submitted to Inlandia prior to his hospitalization and death, we connected with more of René than even we could have ever imagined. He wrote with a profound understanding of human complexities, his characters brimming with flaws, contradictions, and resilience. René saw life in layers, and through this story, he wove together themes of family, love, and belonging with a voice that we knew from years of loving him. René and our mother, Paula, shared a special relationship and closeness, so we're certain that his writing about family was with her in mind. Reading *Search Party*, we felt his presence across every page—his wit, his vulnerability, his insight and his intelligence. Books like this one not only illuminate the world of their characters, but also, offer a window into the soul of their creator. For us, engaging with René's words has been both a celebration, a consolation, and an ongoing conversation with someone we miss so dearly.

By sharing this novel with the world, we honor René's life and his incomparable talent. *Search Party* is not just a story about family—it is also a reflection of the warmth and complexity he brought to his own relationships and of his gift for giving voice to the undercurrents of love, pain, and hope that define us all. Publishing his book allows us to hold René close forever while also letting his vision and artistry take flight, reaching others who, like us, can take comfort and inspiration from his words. We are proud to offer *Search Party* to you, not just as René's family but as admirers of a writer whose work is more relevant and meaningful than ever in today's world. May this book touch your heart as it has touched ours.

—The Solivans

I

O n his fortieth birthday, my son Luis spends the day with me searching for his mother Vinita in the Bronx. Something we've been doing on and off since the day he was born. I watch from my car (an '82 blue Ford Granada with a million miles on it) as Luis walks up to strangers on the Grand Concourse showing them a picture of Vinita. They say things like *She's beautiful* or *I see the resemblance*, shake their heads and move on.

Luis looks up and down the Concourse fanning himself with his mother's picture. Like his father he's a typical Puerto Rican man. Handsome. Dark skin, dark hair, dark eyes. He and I think we're different from other Puerto Ricans, but we're not. Our hands move a lot when we talk and we talk loud. Our emotions erupt easily. Our arguments are often weak but expressed with so much passion that we're often told we're dramatic (though we think we're not).

Unlike me Luis is still trim with a full head of hair. Always turning heads. Even now as he walks up to a store window and stares at sneakers, his tight T-shirt and shorts accenting every muscle on him, catching the eye of passersby, both men and women. I look at my watch. I go to hit the horn then stop because the horn is louder than it needs to be. More suitable for a freight train. I decide to be patient. Let Luis enjoy his window shopping.

Now Luis is in a trance. Frozen in front of a pair of blue sneakers.

As soon as I hit the horn, I regret it. Luis jumps off the ground. The arms go up. Vinita's picture goes flying. The hands cover the head like he was just shot at, the bullet barely missing. He looks at me. He's saying something not very nice. I look away.

Luis gets into the car with Vinita's picture. Instead of sitting in the front seat again, he climbs into the back to teach me a lesson. Because that's what Puerto Ricans do. We teach people lessons. It's our duty.

In the back seat Luis slides across the tan leather like he's expecting his sisters Olivia and Ivonne to slide in next to him. But they won't be sliding in. My daughters broke up our search party some time ago. Olivia went off to write another book. Ivonne escaped the Bronx with her family to live on a farm. We only hear from Olivia when she needs money. Ivonne reaches out through cards. Birthday cards. Anniversary cards. Christmas cards filled with photos of herself, the husband, the son. Their eyes looking up or down or anywhere but the camera. Everyone always wearing something red or green or both. Wearing things like sweaters with reindeers. No one ever looks happy. Yet in her perfect Catholic schoolgirl handwriting, Ivonne carries on about how happy they are on the farm. How different it is from the Bronx. Always ending her notes with the same threat she never follows through on. *We're coming to visit.*

"When are you going to fix the A/C," Luis says. "It's like Death Valley back here. We should go there again."

"I've never been to Death Valley."

"Sure you have. That trip to Vegas a few years ago. We rented a car and drove through Death Valley on our way to California. It was like a thousand degrees."

"Wasn't me."

"Must've been Mami."

"I don't think so."

"It was somebody. Some girl. Ginger maybe—Stop the car."

I hit the brakes and look out the window expecting to see Vinita. All I see is a rundown pizzeria.

"I'm starving," Luis says.

"I thought we'd do something nicer for your birthday."

Luis blows air through his lips like he's five years old and gets out of the car.

Inside the pizzeria I'm dreading it because I hate to watch my son eat. Because he eats his pizza now like he's choking. His head shakes. The neck turns to work the food down and I think he's dying and I say over and over *Are you alright?* And Luis looks at me the same way he did as a boy. Like I'm out of my mind. His eyes begging me to leave him alone.

Luis picks up his pizza and moves to the next table. His back to me. I relax and eat my pizza, wondering where Vinita is.

On the day Luis was born, I held him in a chair while Vinita lay in bed next to us at Morrisania Hospital in the Bronx. She said something about using the bathroom. I think I said *should I get a nurse* as I stared at baby Luis. By the time I looked up, she was gone. For the next twenty minutes or so, I followed a nurse around with Luis in my arms. Up and down corridors, stairwells. Searching for his mother. We found Vinita in her hospital gown, barefoot on the ground floor. Arguing with a security guard who was refusing to let her leave the building. A scenario that has been playing out in various forms ever since.

Luis and I walk along the Grand Concourse between Fordham and Kingsbridge Road. We walk through a park.

We stop in front of a place Vinita and I used to visit often. The Poe Cottage. Which isn't really a cottage but *a farmhouse built in 1812* the tour guide said every time we took the tour. Often we were the only ones on the tour and the guide knew we knew every detail, but he'd tell us again. *This is the place where Edgar Allan Poe wrote many of his great works. Where he spent his final years. Where his wife Virginia died.*

It's Saturday, but the first floor of the cottage is empty except for a male employee reading a book. I turn down his offer for a guided tour.

He returns to his book.

"What are we doing here?" Luis says.

I tell him his mother loves this place. Loves staring at everything for hours. The table Poe wrote at. The chair Virginia sat on. The bed they made love in. The bed I found Vinita staring at a year ago and the year before that.

We move into the roped-off kitchen area. The table is set for two.

"Don't you love that, Luis?"

"What?"

"The way the old china is placed. Like the Poes have just gone into another room and at any moment will return."

"This is a sad place with sad spirits. I'm getting all sorts of signs—"

"Stop, just...stop."

Up the old wooden stairs we go. Each step met with a grating creak.

We pop our heads into a room with a blue desk, the paint peeling, the wood underneath distressed.

"This is where Poe wrote," I say.

"Wonderful." Luis looks at his watch.

Then we're in the bedroom standing in front of the Poes' bed, no sign of Vinita.

"The bed is where it all happens," I say.

"Here we go." Luis sighs, shakes his head.

"Where you talk about everything and nothing. Where you listen to each other breathe after the lovemaking ends, your nose buried in her back, inhaling her scent, waiting for sleep to arrive..."

"Why are you crying?"

"Because this is where the Poes made love, where Virginia lay when she got sick. When she died, Poe stood right here or maybe sat over there in a chair and watched Virginia take her last breath and the room got quiet except for some noise outside the window—maybe a horse carriage going by at the exact moment this bed became a coffin—and isn't that the saddest thing in the world?"

2

When I decided, months ago, that I wanted nothing to do with men anymore, my father suggested a dog. *You need a dog Olivia,* he said. *You need to take care of something other than yourself,* he was always saying, referring to kids, but when I didn't take the hint, he moved on to dogs and I thought dogs would be a lot less trouble, but dogs have to be walked three times a day, I read, and the idea of having to walk three times a day in the brutal cold of the Bronx was too much for me so I opted for a cat, one I saw in a pet store window on the Grand Concourse near Fordham Road. This sleepy kitten—a grey Turkish Angora—who later, in my ground-floor apartment, emerged wide awake from his travel cage, took one look at my new hair color, Clairol's Nice n' Easy #8: Champagne Blonde, hissed then disappeared into the living room. By that evening I had returned to my natural hair color, a dull burnt umber. For the next three days, the cat hissed at me, even scratched my ankles a few times, showing no interest in being taken care of. Fuck this. I decided to return the cat to the pet store, but he had no intention of leaving, hiding under the sofa or bed or behind this or that every time

I came towards him with the travel cage. My father kept offering to come over and catch the cat, but I'd say *no, no, I can do it,* but I couldn't, not today, so I surrendered and called my father and said *please come over and get this Turkish beast out of here,* then there was an explosion outside, a car backfiring perhaps. I flinched. A plate slipped out of my hand, shattering in the kitchen sink. The cat looked up at me from his food bowl and I swear he mumbled something, sounded like *fuck you, lady* and it was those three words I kept hearing that day, staring ahead at a brick wall covered in bare vines, dry and brittle. This was what I saw from the sole window in my new office, the smallest room in the world. There was a desk, a chair, a trashcan. The office was temporary until another one, a bigger one, became available, he said, an older man standing before me. His lips were moving, but I had no idea what he was saying or who he was, or I knew who he was but couldn't remember. There was no heat. I hadn't taken off my coat since I got there, rubbing my hands together the whole time, staring at the man still chattering, standing in the doorway wearing a coat that was way too big for him. He smelled like parmesan cheese or vomit. He informed me now that the office had just been painted, that these lilac/pink walls were called Mulberry Bliss as if this information was supposed to lift my spirits—it didn't—and what the hell was his name, something Lock or Lockly or Lockney—yes, Lockney, the Chair of the English Department.

"The color is lovely, Dr. Lockney."

Lockney asked if I had seen the semester's schedule, and before I could answer, a schedule appeared and he began to read it to me line by line, slowly, as if I were eight years old. I looked at him, nodding as I tried to remember the last time I punched a clock, at least a year, definitely a year, a year of living modestly on the advance for my second novel until it dried up, forcing me to ask my parents if I could move back in with them so I could write, but they said *no,* said I should go back to retail, that the Sears near them was hiring. Then I said *no.* Mami brought up my various degrees and suggested I teach like her sister Lourdes the Professor. When I reminded her that Aunt Lourdes was always miserable whenever we saw her, Mami told me it'd be perfect for me.

"Olivia, you have lots of degrees," Lockney had said, months ago, during my interview. "However—except for some undergraduate writing courses taught in graduate school—you have no real teaching experience. But you have a *New York Times* bestseller. We've never had a professor with one of those." A month later Lockney offered me a position teaching writing, and even though I was broke, I didn't want the job anymore, opting to borrow money from my parents again who turned me down as gently as my father could: "Olivia, we have no more money to give you. So you can either go back to Macy's and fold sweaters all day or you can grow up. You're forty-five. Take the goddamn job."

Lockney stopped reading and pushed the schedule across my little desk.

"And once you submit your grades, you're done for the semester."

Lockney stared out my little window for some time then looked back at me and didn't seem to know who I was, looking around in a panic as though he had just realized he was standing at the wrong bus stop. As soon as he was gone, I felt a loneliness jab at my heart like it often did late at night. I went to the doorway and there was no one around except Lockney at the end of the hall about to turn a corner. I called his name and asked if he wanted to get some coffee, then we were sitting at a nearby Starbucks, the place nearly empty, *for now*, Lockney said, *but next week it will be a madhouse when the students arrive*. Small talk occurred for some time and it was an effort for me until his wedding ring caught my eye. I must've asked about it, about his marriage, because he said *twenty-eight years*, and I thought *wow*, but I must've said it out loud too because he said, "No, no, no. No wow, not anymore. In the early years of marriage, yes, lots of wow moments but now...no."

Lockney reached across the table and placed his hand on mine, said I could call him Will, never Bill, his hand warmer than I expected. I contemplated the gesture, trying to determine if it was appropriate or not. Maybe he cared. Maybe this is how people you don't meet online act. I didn't find him attractive, but if I squinted, I sort of, kind of, thought he was distinguished enough to sleep with and *how typical of you*, Papi would say later, *to want to sleep with your boss—again—I mean really, Olivia, what good did that do for you last time with what's his name at Macy's—you tell me way too much, stop telling me things, I'm your father, damnit, not your girlfriend.*

My hand slipped away from Lockney's. Words were exchanged. How I had to get back, then I was in it, my office, standing in the middle of the room taking in the space, the walls, the Mulberry Bliss; the little yellow telephone on my desk that seemed from another time. I wondered if it worked and it did and I checked my voice messages at home, one from my father explaining how he wasn't coming over to deal with my cat, that he couldn't spend time chasing a four-legged devil around my apartment, because my mother Vinita went missing again today and would I like to join him and my brother Luis in the search. Then Papi thanked me for forgetting his birthday and there was no irony in his voice and this made me sad. It was my mother who kept track of birthdays and anniversaries, who called us seven days in advance, to make sure my siblings and I bought and mailed a card because we were a "card" family. No calls or emails for us. It had to be something you could *feel* in your hand, my mother always said. But there was no reminder call from her this week. It had been a while since I bought a card or maybe I had and forgot, either way I don't like cards anymore.

I stood on a subway platform calling my father to wish him *Happy Birthday*. No answer. A call came in from my agent, Tom. My book editor—Mason—called. He's emailing notes, it's all good, he loves the draft but what's up with the writer character, he knows nothing about her, about *you*, reveal yourself because he likes the rest of the characters, loves that you decided to go down the memoir route.

"It's not a memoir, Tom," I said into the phone, pacing the platform. "Why would he think it's a memoir?"

"Because one of the characters is a nameless writer from the Bronx like you."

"I know lots of nameless writers from the Bronx—it's not a memoir."

"Olivia, please..."

"What?"

"I've heard many of your family stories over drinks and dinners.

With you in tears most of the time. And I've met some of your family members and I see them in this book. And the last one. Just because you changed their names doesn't make it fiction."

The subway platform was getting crowded. I opened my mouth to say something, but nothing came out.

"Mason said they've had meetings about it, about marketing the book as a memoir, assuming that's the way you want to go."

"No—"

"Don't answer now, give it some thought, I mean, they're not going to force you. It's just that they had another memoir they were excited about, then they had to put the brakes on it. Some scandal with the author. But I can tell them it's fiction."

"Thank you."

"I just thought it would be good for you to explore another genre."

"Tom, a memoir is like signing another contract."

"What contract?"

"The one that says I have to stick to the truth, that I can't make shit up."

"Oh please, you don't think memoir writers make shit up? They all do, they have to. As a reader I assume that, I mean, there's no way they could possibly remember *everything*, every detail..."

A train was arriving on the opposite track. Tom presented an argument about memoirs. I was about to say *no* when I heard the words *play well* over and over in my head. My mother had been telling me to play well since I was a little girl, the words whispered to me every time I started a new school, a new job, a new relationship. But I never learned how to play well, my box often checked, the one that said *Doesn't play well with others*. Checked by teachers, bosses, boyfriends, my first husband who I always mentioned whenever I went on a date because I didn't want my dates to think that I had never been wanted, didn't want them to think things like *You're forty-five years old, why are you still single, what is wrong with you?* And I'd say to these dates, casually, *I was married a long time ago, but it didn't work out, very messy, all of it, the marriage, the divorce*; a confession that always made my dates squirm but made me feel as though I wasn't the last doll on the shelf no one wanted to play with.

The train was pulling into the platform. Tom was talking about Joan Didion's *The Year of Magical Thinking* when I said something into the phone, something like *I'll think about it* while a group of strangers swept me into a crowded train.

Back at my apartment building, I stood outside looking for my mother. Over the years there were times I'd find her in the alleyway of my apartment buildings drinking a Diet Coke while sitting on her blue suitcase from another time. But not tonight.

Inside the apartment a glass of Pinot Noir was poured. I roamed the apartment searching for the cat, expecting to be hissed or scratched at every corner. Then, in the living room, I heard a bell toy slamming into things as if the cat were playing soccer. I shook my head. Moments later I was in the bedroom sitting at my desk, wine glass in hand, reading my editor's notes.

Then I wrote for some time, abandoning fiction, treating it all as memoir. Writing about me, my life in my twenties. I read it out loud and none of it worked so I started again and again. This went on for hours until I couldn't focus because I could hear the bell toy in the other room, the sound growing louder, and it felt as if someone was digging an ice pick into my last nerve.

I went to the living room. The cat abandoned the bell toy and ran off. I picked it up and threw it in the hallway closet.

Then I wrote. Wrote well into my third week at the university where I had developed a routine: In between my classes, I'd sit in my little office on my little chair working on my "memoir" then taking breaks to grade student essays with the help of an egg timer Lockney had given me. He told me not to spend more than eight minutes on each essay, to focus on the students' understanding of the rhetorical situation, their critical thinking skills or lack thereof; not to bother commenting on grammar or punctuation but that was all I could comment on because I didn't know what I was doing, especially when it came to my creative writing students' *works*, I called them, not *stories*, for they were not stories yet. Mostly a mishmash of trivial nonsense like the kind I used to write at their age about teenage angst and love lost and found and lost again and again. It wasn't long before I was having serious time management issues, unable to keep up with the work, the reading, the grading. Partly because my heart wasn't int it, partly because I was consumed with my "memoir," the deadline hanging over my head like a fucking guillotine.

"I don't know what I'm doing wrong," I said one day to Lockney.

We were having dinner in a restaurant far from the campus.

"Give it time, Olivia. You'll catch on."

For two months I had been meeting Lockney for lunch once a week, waiting for my heart to race the way he said his heart races every time he sees me. My left foot was trapped now between his brown Oxfords. I looked into his eyes, once again, waiting to feel something.

Anything.

I pulled my foot away and Lockney looked disappointed and I knew right there that it wouldn't be long now before he checked the box (*Doesn't play well with others*) and ran away. I felt myself about to cry and looked out the window, my eyes fixed on a hummingbird fluttering against the glass. I tapped lightly on the window, startling the bird, and watched it fly away. I didn't notice Lockney pay the check and leave, because I was still searching for the hummingbird even while I sat back at my apartment, by the bedroom window, convinced the bird had followed me home. I got up from the window and sat in front of my computer feeling very uncomfortable as if I were on a blind date and we had run out of things to say. For weeks it had been a challenge to find that line between fiction and memoir, mostly due to my age and by that I mean my memory is not what it once was. This is supposed to be a memoir—intentionally now—filled with the truth, but what if you can't remember the truth? What do you do? Fill in the gaps with lies then fight with your publisher to label the book a semi-autobiography so you're not called a fraud? Or do you make yourself inconsequential to the story, more like a piece of furniture than a person, so you don't have to reveal yourself and move on to other characters and events that are etched in old memories that are as clear as glass? Or worse, what if some days your memory doesn't fail you, but what you *do* remember is not as compelling as you thought when you read it on paper? Like my marriage. Dull, loveless, routine. A life between two people who had nothing in common except the desire to be married, to anyone, before they were twenty-five. I wrote that part of my life as it was, barely remembering any details, feeling guilty every time I found myself filling in the blanks with embellishments. I called Tom, and when he didn't answer, I sent him text messages about my struggles with the truth, that I'm going to ditch the memoir idea, return to the comforts of fiction. An hour later he responded. He was still struggling with his new Nokia phone, with the whole texting thing, unable to control his fingers, accidentally sending texts before they were ready. I got used to his texts arriving in groups of three or more:

*don't get stuck*
*on the truth*
*a memoir*
*is as factual*
*as memory permits*

And with that I wrote freely for days.

Then one Saturday afternoon I noticed something unusual...

*(Quiet)*

I got up and walked through the apartment searching for the cat who was always making some kind of noise, disruption. I was convinced the cat never slept, his insomnia born out of his obsession to torture me. After more failed attempts at getting him into the travel cage, I began leaving windows open in hopes that he'd get the hint and move on. It's the ground floor, I told myself, he can't get hurt jumping from the ground floor. I wanted to call his name but couldn't because I had never given him a name.

I went into the kitchen and pressed the electric can opener. The little motor roared. I stared at the kitchen doorway. No cat. I pressed the can opener again and left my hand on it. An hour later the sun had set, shadows had shifted, and I was still standing in the kitchen, in the dark, my hand on the can opener, the motor roaring, thinking about the cat all night and all the next day as I walked the halls of the university unaware of anything and anyone, my mind preoccupied with the cat (*Where did he go, is he eating, the hell with him*). Moving down empty stairwells I was convinced the cat had entered, singing "Wild Horses" by the Rolling Stones until I exited a stairwell and found myself on the side of the building, turning a corner and bumping into Lockney surrounded by a few of our colleagues. Greetings were exchanged. Lockney instructed the other professors to go on ahead.

"How are you, Olivia?"

I forced a smile and gave a small nod.

"We're going to celebrate my birthday at Charley's," he said. "It's not until this weekend but...join us."

"I can't. My mother had been...away...but my father said she came back last night so I'm going to go see her—"

"One drink."

I looked up at the grey skies and planned my evening: *wine, laundry, writing, see who's online.* I fought back the urge to cry and nodded.

"But I have to go buy you a birthday card."

"That's not necessary."

"No, no, no, my mother always said you can't celebrate someone's birthday without giving them a card. It's bad luck or something. Go. I'll see you there." Then, as if he had read my mind, Lockney moved closer and gave me a hug. I wanted him to never let go, and when he did, I watched him cross the street, suddenly grateful that I hadn't slept with him. But it was coming. Not now though. Maybe in the summer when school was out and I needed errands and people to fill my days.

I walked a few blocks to a pharmacy that sold greeting cards. I choose a card with blue on it. *Get a card with blue on it*, my mother always said. *I read somewhere blue makes people feel good.*

On my way to the register, I passed by the make up counter and stopped in front of a large round mirror and looked at my reflection. There was more of everything than I expected. More wrinkles, more weight, more grey hair. Ten minutes later I walked out of the pharmacy without a birthday card and headed home. Buried in a plastic bag held close to my chest was a box of Clairol's Nice n' Easy #8: Champagne Blonde.

As soon as I got home, I opened the living room windows. I leaned out one, then the other, hoping for a glimpse of the cat. I poured myself a glass of wine and drank it in front of the cat's double feeder, both bowls empty. I called up my father and told him the cat was gone. He said *thank God* and I worked hard to sound as pleased as he was. I asked to speak to my mother.

"Your mother's gone again," Papi said.

When I hung up the phone, I wandered from the kitchen to the living room, sipping on wine, composing a to-do list in my head: *vacuum cat hair, throw out litter box, dye hair.*

And there was the cat sitting on a windowsill.

I froze with the wine glass on my lips, afraid to move. The cat jumped into the living room and went into the kitchen with me behind him. He went to the double feeder and sniffed the empty bowls. The cat came towards me and rubbed against my legs then went back to the feeder and rubbed against it, purring the whole time. I put the wine glass down and retrieved a can of cat food. When the can opener roared, the cat's purring grew louder. I dumped food in one bowl, water in the other. I watched him eat, thinking of names for him. Sebastian. Oliver. Tobias. I squatted next to the cat then reached out to pet him. He pulled away, hissed and scratched my hand. I backed away and stood there sipping on wine, watching him. Waiting until the cat was done. Waiting to see if he needed anything else.

In the bathroom, I held my scratched hand under warm water then dried it. On the edge of the sink sat the box of Clairol. It was picked up and tossed in the trash. At the bathroom doorway I looked around and saw the cat lying at the end of the hallway licking his paw. He looked at me for a second then continued licking. I went to the hallway closet and searched inside until I found the bell toy then tossed it towards the cat. It landed a few inches from him. The cat looked at the toy without interest and continued licking his paw. I went into the bedroom. Stood there for a long time staring at old family photos on the wall. I sat at my computer and rewrote my life as fiction and it was a happier one. My marriage filled with love and passion, past mistakes averted, more friends than I could imagine. I stopped writing when I began to laugh, not sure why, the wine maybe. I deleted everything I had just written and started over, pushing myself to the background, focusing on the others, the family, *my* family, every single one hanging by a thread. And when I heard the sound of the bell toy in the hallway, I closed my eyes and listened and I swear it sounded like music.

## 3

Not far from the Poe Cottage my son lives in a walk-up apartment. A walk-up apartment is a nice way of saying this building has no elevator so prepare to walk up a lot of fucking stairs.

Luis is in his apartment now using the bathroom. I'm waiting out front in the Granada double parked. He seemed confused I wasn't going up with him. When I reminded him that I had used the bathroom at the pizzeria, Luis said, "You're sixty-seven. Don't you have to go like every five minutes?"

I probably could've squeezed out a few drops. But my legs told me we aren't doing any stairs.

This is Luis' third apartment in five years. He's had twice as many jobs in the same period. He gets bored quickly. He told Vinita he took this apartment because it was close to Lehman College. He attended classes there then stopped. His mother asked why. We all asked why. But he wouldn't say. I'm sure it was something simple. Like someone looked at him the wrong way. Said the wrong thing and that was that. A few months ago, he completed an online program in para-something, I forget. Having to do with communicating with the dead, something he's been doing since he was a boy without our support or encouragement. And I say communicating—not talking—to the dead because, apparently, when we die, we don't talk, we use signs, Luis says, and each sign means something like the letters in the alphabet. He recently started a business, helping people contact the dead, their loved ones that have long gone to that place where no one has a voice anymore. Anyway, Luis' new business must not be doing well.

He's always asking everyone for loans he never pays back. He works at a bank too. Or used to work at a bank. I think this week he works at the front desk of a gym—I don't know where my son works.

Luis gets into the car. Into the front seat this time.

"I called Ivonne last night," Luis says. "I needed money, but I didn't want to tell her I needed money until the time was right so I pretended I wanted to talk about Mami losing her memory and what should we do about her because you're useless, Papi."

"Your mother's not losing her memory."

"I know that, but Ivonne's on a goddamn farm, she doesn't know anything. She said Mami losing her memory would be a good thing then wished she herself was losing her memory so that it could all be wiped out, our past. Then she started going on about Uma Thurman in some movie, how turned on she was by her, how she wished she were gay. Wouldn't that be better for me, Ivonne said, to be gay instead of always waiting around for another man to fuck up my life, *again*, and she said *again* like it had ten syllables, her voice *reeeeal sloooow* like she was running out of batteries. And when I asked her about her son, Ivonne said she didn't want to talk about him, then she talked about him, how he keeps stealing her credit cards and going off on trips. She let him have it the other night when he returned to the farm from Puerto Rico. *I told him that trips are earned around here*, she said, *not awarded, this isn't The Fucking Price Is Right*. Then her son gave her the evil eye, she said, and called her a *Chupacabra*, a mystical creature, he explained, a goatsucker rumored to roam the island of Puerto Rico sucking the life out of everything it touched. And Ivonne didn't know what pissed her off more. That her son called her a *Chupacabra* or that he felt the need to explain what the creature was like she was some moron, like she didn't stay up-to-date with Puerto Rican mythology and *pleeeease* let's not talk about my son, she said, let's talk about something else because she felt her blood pressure rising. Then I heard rattling over the phone. It sounded like pills in a pill bottle then the sound of running water. She cleared her throat and asked how I was and we began to talk about asparagus and the antioxidants in green tea—"

I turn on the radio. Real loud. Some oldies station. A song I like but I don't know the name, sung by Frank Sinatra or Tony Bennett, I can never tell them apart.

Luis says, "Why do you think Mami keeps running away?"

I don't say anything. Luis repeats his question louder because he thinks I didn't hear him.

"I don't know why she keeps running away," I say.

"When I was a kid, she was always going off to California, for the movies, she'd say but I figured Mami left because she was never into it."

"Into what?"

"Being a mother."

"That's not true."

"Sure it is. Mami always acted like those workers at the movie theatres she'd take me and Olivia and Ivonne to, you know, the ones selling popcorn and candy. Bored out of their minds like they were just there killing time until something better came along."

My eyes are on the red traffic light in front of me. Thinking of that time Vinita and I spent in Las Vegas. Hanging out in smoky casinos. Watching quarters fall out of slot machines when quarters used to fall out of slot machines. Sipping on vodka tonics until someone said something about downtown. *Have you seen downtown? You gotta go downtown. The slot machines are so loose.* So we took a cab downtown. Neon flashing everywhere. Billboards zipping by of old singers we thought were dead. Laughing until it hurt.

"But me and Olivia and Ivonne moved out years ago," Luis says. "I think Mami runs away now because she doesn't like you—"

"Get out!"

"Papi—"

"We're here. Get out. So I can park."

With Vinita's picture in hand, Luis gets out of the car in front of the Loew's Paradise Theatre on the Grand Concourse. I find a parking spot a few feet away. I watch Luis through the rearview mirror. Walking up to strangers. Holding Vinita's picture between them. I get out of the car to stretch my legs. I look at the entrance of the theatre. The whole building closed for renovations. This is where we found Vinita when she ran away last year or the year before.

Sitting in front of the theatre on her blue suitcase. In tears. Sad that this once glorious movie house had been butchered. Turned into a multi-screen mess by some corporation. It was here in the fifties where Vinita and I held hands in the dark every Saturday night. Sitting in red velvet seats stained and torn. Waiting for the movie to start. Our heads looking up through a cloud of cigarette smoke. At a ceiling that looked like the night sky with tiny lights twinkling like stars and maybe Luis is right, maybe Vinita doesn't like me *now*, but she did then. I know she did.

We'd stroll out of the theatre holding hands, looking the best we ever looked. Always stopping for a kiss. *Always.* Then she'd pull away and stare at a movie poster of Grace Kelly or Marilyn Monroe and she'd mimic their pose and we'd laugh.

But today Vinita is not outside the theatre.

Luis is entering a bakery. A few minutes later he is sitting in the back seat with a cupcake in hand.

I start the car. I check the rearview mirror for traffic. I notice Luis staring at the cupcake. He begins to sing "Happy Birthday" to himself. Quietly. I want to sing with him, but I don't. I don't want to be asked again why I am crying.

# 4

When the sunlight arrived on the island, it moved through their house like ghosts, flooding her mother's tidy rooms with warm light. In that moment the *coquíes* would stop singing, and their house would come back to life, aided by the smell that rose from the coffee fields behind their house. Every morning Vinita and her family would sit at the breakfast table, and she would wish she wasn't eleven but old enough to drink coffee, *this* coffee, Puerto Rico's finest. She and her sister Lourdes had tasted it once from a half-filled cup of coffee their mother, Dolores, had left behind one morning. They never forgot the taste. Or how alive and alert they felt afterwards.

On a windowsill Vinita caught a glimpse of a grey lizard lounging in the shade that vanished so quickly she wondered if it had even been there. She ate her breakfast, studying the morning light, the way it softened the lines around her father's eyes, the way it lengthened her mother's shadow as she fussed over her family.

Vinita and Lourdes loved living on a coffee plantation. Loved helping their father pick beans and the way their fingers smelled afterwards. When their friends came over, they would drag them through the coffee fields, telling them everything they knew about coffee. Like how the best way to plant the coffee, to ensure the best bean, the best flavor, was to put seven seeds in a hole at the beginning of the rainy season—and not a moment sooner—or the beans would not change colors when roasted, their father Gabriel would say. And they *must* change colors so they can be labeled: *light, medium, dark, very dark.*

Years later, with their father long gone, the sisters often heard his words, his voice, low and gravelly, whispering in their ears. *Light, medium, dark, very dark.* Vinita would hear him whenever she was at a Bronx market selecting coffee from the many flavors and brands. While Lourdes heard her father's words in the mornings, like today, sitting across from her husband, Javier, at their kitchen table as she stared into her coffee, examining the color, claiming to herself that it was dark, then very dark, yes, Papi would call this *very dark.* She sipped on her coffee and wondered, as she often did, how she ended up marrying a Puerto Rican who didn't drink coffee.

"How's your tea?" Lourdes said.

"The movie's at 4:00," Javier said. The top of his head was peaking up from *The New York Times.* "I'll meet you in front of the Film Forum at 3:45. The tea's fine."

"I have to make an appearance at a retirement party at 7:00."

He assured her that she'd be out of the movie in time.

"You can come to the party if you want."

"I don't want."

Lourdes held her nose over her cup, inhaled then said, "What movie?"

"*Love Story,*" he said, setting the paper down on the table.

"What's it called?" she said.

"*Love Story.* Ryan O'Neal, Ali MacGraw."

Lourdes poured herself another cup of coffee and considered suggesting another movie, a current movie, *anything* made in this decade. Javier was a retired history professor who was trapped in the past, willingly. Current topics didn't interest him. Current films interested him even less.

Lourdes opened her mouth, paused, then closed it, regretting having told him years ago that she hadn't seen the film, this *Love Story*. Vinita had told her it was a sad film, a *tearjerker*, and oh how Lourdes despised that word; the whole idea of having her tears jerked out of her really pissed her off and Javier knew this, knew how she avoided these films, but he was determined to see one with her to see her cry. After twenty-nine years of marriage, Javier had never seen Lourdes cry and he knew she cried often. He could see it in her eyes, often red and swollen. He would try to comfort her but she'd wave him off, insisting it was her allergies. And on days when Lourdes cried—and there were many—she would secure an isolated place, a closet, a pantry, an empty subway car or her favorite, a running shower. Only once, when they were first married, did Javier walk in on her. She was standing in the shower crying silently when he joined her, aroused. He made love to her while she cried the whole time, hiding her tears under the spray of warm water. *He never noticed*, she had told Vinita. And why would he. Lourdes and Vinita had become masters at burying their tears at an early age, twelve to be exact, the year their father died in bed, not his bed, a neighbor's, a very pretty one. Their mother refused to cry for her unfaithful husband, demanding the same from her daughters, their tears met with lashings. By the time they sat at their father's funeral surrounded by teary friends and relatives, Vinita and Lourdes remained like their mother. Stoic, dry-eyed, bored. As if they were waiting for a bus.

"Can we see another movie?" Lourdes said. "There's something playing with Debbie Reynolds."

"I love *Singing in the Rain*. Actually it's *Singin' in the Rain*. The g is—"

"Something new. Just came out last month."

Javier riffled through the newspaper.

"Vinita said it's funny, light. You know, she met Debbie Reynolds in Hollywood way back when at some party."

"*Mother*," Javier said.

"Hmm?"

"The movie. It's called *Mother*."

Javier pointed to a movie ad with Debbie Reynolds and Albert Brooks. Lourdes stood up and looked over his shoulder at the ad.

"That's it."

She reached for a wool scarf folded over a chair, this long ivory thing, its edges adorned with coffee stains that always reminded her to wash the damn thing though she never did. Her eyes slid from the movie ad to Javier's head, to his bald spot guarded by strands of curly grey hair, hair she had come to accept. She missed when it was dark and thick. It was the first thing she'd noticed, his hair, when she saw him in the main library of Columbia University. She was an undergraduate student (a senior), he was a professor specializing in Latin History. And though she'd had crushes on professors in the past, this one was different, *he* was different. He was the youngest professor on staff, and he wasn't a Smith or a Stein or a Brown, no, he was a Ramos, and he was dark and exotic. She enrolled in one of his classes simply to be near him. His Latin History class bored her, but he did not. There was an intoxicating bravado to his teaching style that she admired, one she would try to imitate years later in her own classes with little success.

"Aren't you going to eat something?" Javier said, nibbling on a piece of dry toast.

In the foyer Lourdes put on a grey, wool coat. A cold breeze caressed her neck. She turned and found the basement door ajar. Lourdes moaned at the thought of Javier sitting down there in his bathrobe in the cold. On restless nights he'd sit in the basement going through their history, preserved everywhere you looked. Shelves crammed with souvenirs from various trips. Boxes everywhere filled with old photos that had never made it into photo albums. *You have to come down here and see this*, he'd often yell up to Lourdes when he'd find an old photo that would stir him up. But Lourdes never went down to the basement; the dampness was not kind to her hair and the fluorescent light made her skin look sickly, green. Then there were the small windows where the glass had been painted black by the previous owners. Natural light never entered the room and Lourdes *loved* natural light. She refused to go down to the basement until Javier scraped the paint off of the glass, a task he had yet to take on.

"You left the basement door open again," she yelled.

"How about pancakes?" Javier yelled back. "I can make pancakes, you want pancakes?"

Lourdes looked down the basement steps. She could see them, partially, the old school desks stacked up against the blackboard, items Javier had picked up in Puerto Rico, years ago, from the schoolhouse he had attended as a child. He had given the school a sizable donation to help rebuild it after a violent storm. They named a small, two-story building after Javier and gave him the old desks and blackboard, per his request. When Lourdes found out later that the shipping of these items—from the island to the States—cost them almost as much as his donation, she tried to set them on fire. Or at least she wanted to.

"I can make you an egg white scramble," Javier said.

"I'll pick up a scone in the city," Lourdes said, closing the basement door.

In the foyer mirror she watched the old professor shuffle through the kitchen doorway, dig into the refrigerator and pull out the butter, the *real* stuff, the stuff he wasn't supposed to have. She knew then that Javier thought she had already left the house without saying goodbye again, an accusation that had been greeting her lately whenever she returned home.

"The low-cholesterol stuff," she yelled, "is behind the cranberry juice."

Javier turned to her, startled, as if she had just caught him pissing in the sink. He put the butter back, sat down and ate his toast dry. In the mirror she studied the old professor. His face resembled a worn stone etched with deep, dark lines. Lately he looked dirty even after a shower. This slovenly look intrigued her when she first met him. Now it just annoyed her.

"I know you're not leaving the house today," she'd often say, "but would it kill you to comb your hair?"

When she'd met him, she noticed right away that he didn't dress like the other professors, the ones that paraded the campus in dull shades of greys and beiges. He dressed like an artist. Lots of colors. And wrinkles. Like someone who didn't own an iron. Lourdes was certain Dr. Javier Ramos wasn't a painter, but she still imagined him painting in the nude, imagined his body being as toned and hairy as the arms that hung out from his short-sleeve shirts. She flirted with him all semester, but it wasn't until she graduated that he agreed to meet at Mirth, her favorite coffee shop, a hole in the wall on 106th and Broadway filled with creative types writing in notebooks, reading, cigarettes hanging from their lips.

"Is that a six or an eight?" Javier said, squinting, holding the newspaper closer.

"Put your glasses on."

Lourdes picked up her bag and thought about Mirth and what a silly name that had been for a coffeehouse. Mirth. A word she had never heard or seen since college when she had to read Wharton's *The House of Mirth* for some English class. A word she felt should not be used unless one wanted to come off as pretentious and this old coffee shop was anything but pretentious with its questionable art and wobbly chrome tables and chrome chairs, their seats and backs covered in burgundy vinyl. It broke her heart years ago when a corporate monster ate up the place then spat it out like something out of *The Body Snatchers*, transforming Mirth into something cold and modern and slick, indistinguishable from its siblings that lived on almost every other block, that wore the same outfit; a green canopy with bold white letters that spelled *Starbucks Coffee*.

"What are you doing this morning?" Lourdes said.

"Stuff," Javier said.

"Stuff?"

"Stuff."

From the start their conversations were either painfully strained or exhilaratingly combative. She couldn't wait for him to pick her up for their dates; by the end of the night, she wanted nothing to do with him. She learned to embrace these extremes once they slept together. She was not surprised that he turned out to be a passionate lover. After all he was Puerto Rican, it was expected. There was a rampant ferocity in their lovemaking that she had never experienced. They did it everywhere. In private places and not-so-private places, tearing into each other like jackals. And unlike her younger lovers, students mostly, Dr. Javier Ramos was not into talking after sex or showing affection. He didn't even like to cuddle. She liked that.

"Where are my glasses?" Javier said.

Lourdes reached into the left pocket of Javier's robe, pulled out a pair of scratched bifocals and slid them onto his face. He scanned the movie listings again and asked, "*Love Story* or *Mother*?" Then he reached for his pill case and studied the letters: S M T W T F S.

"It's Thursday," Lourdes said. When Javier reached for the wrong compartment, she offered, "The second T."

He opened the Thursday compartment and took his pills. He placed a hand on his large belly and moved it in a circular motion. He wasn't wearing his usual flannel pajama top, she noticed, but a Hawaiian shirt, the red and turquoise one, the one from their Santa Fe trip before they were married, the one Javier wore in the desert when they pretended to be strangers and he pushed her on a rock and had his way with her and she liked the way the blood galloped through her, leaving her breathless, dizzy, insane. The moment seemed historic to him, like a famous battle, a reenactment of the conquest of the Aztecs by the Spanish led by General Javier Ramos, who stood there now in triumph, his Hawaiian shirt fluttering in the wind like a flag of victory.

"*Love Story*," Javier said, pushing his pill case away.

Lourdes was about to make a case for *Mother* when Javier repeated the movie title, his movie, to himself as if she had already left the room.

"I'll be in front of the Film Forum at 11:45," she said.

Lourdes repeated herself, twice more, until Javier acknowledged her with a nod. She looked out the window, adjusting her scarf. The wind was blowing hard, keeping yesterday's snow in motion. Smoke rose from their neighbor's chimney, bled into the sky then mocked a cluster of clouds. Lourdes took a sip of coffee. She looked at Javier staring into the newspaper, intensely, his lips moving, his face contorted as if preparing for a sneeze that never came. She knew there was no point in disturbing him now with trivial things like how his newspaper was upside down. She kissed him goodbye and—for a brief moment—was annoyed he never noticed.

# 5

Vinita stepped off the bus on 5th Avenue and allowed herself to be swept up by the afternoon crowd, riding it until she arrived at an entrance to Central Park. She entered the park with her head down to keep the wind out of her eyes. At sixty-seven, Vinita still walked with the brisk pace of a much younger woman. She loved this walk, the way it relieved the tension buried in her bones; the way the sounds of nature fought to be heard over the traffic and sirens and music coming from boom boxes or street musicians. Nothing bothered her now. Not even the wind and cold tugging at her from all sides like children wanting to play. Her path was crowded with tourists speaking foreign languages, some holding cameras while others posed for pictures.

Vinita continued walking until the crowds thinned out. She stopped at an empty bench, brushed the snow away with a gloved hand and sat down. All sorts of thoughts and concerns suddenly appeared before her, only to be banished with a wave of a hand. She took a deep breath, looked around. The snow had claimed everything. A horse and carriage went by carrying a man and woman bundled up in bright colors. A bird, a little fluffy brown thing, landed on the bench and perused her.

"I have nothing for you," she said.

As if understanding her, the bird skipped to the edge of the bench and took off. Her eyes followed its path until the sun blinded her. Vinita moved her scarf up over her nose then studied the sunlight, the way it drew colors out of everything it touched, the same way she had studied it as a girl when she lived on the island. She liked when the light was sharp, brilliant, falling like stardust on the heads of children climbing mango trees. Sometimes the light was dull and indifferent, rude even, forcing her to run and hide from it. On rare occasions the light seemed to be in the most glorious mood, making everyone it touched look beautiful. Love traveled in this light, Vinita believed; it lived, slept and wept there. Then by nightfall, she would forget about the light and become intrigued by the dark that assembled in the stones and the cracks in all shades of grey like the concrete floor she now stood on at Starbucks. A barista handed her a coffee and apologized for the wait.

Vinita walked to the front of the Starbucks and slid into an overstuffed chair covered in purple velvet. She sipped on her coffee as she stared out the window. When it began to rain, she made a face at the snow already getting slushy, making the street slippery. Suddenly umbrellas seemed to magically appear everywhere, moving by like a dream, like that wild umbrella dance she and Cruz had taken Luis to see when they were on a trip to Los Angeles; a Cirque du Soleil show inside a tent on the Santa Monica Pier. The thought of Los Angeles brought tears to her eyes, which she quickly wiped away when she saw her sister approach.

"Sorry I'm late," Lourdes said.

She dropped her bag in the chair across from Vinita. Placed her coffee down on the small table between them, her coat over the back of her chair. Lourdes examined Vinita with a quick glance, noticed she had gained weight but said nothing.

They sat there quietly for some time sipping on coffee, staring out the window.

"How's your girl doing?" Vinita said.

"Better now that we both have mobile phones. Though there is less of a need for her to come see us anymore. She's no longer knocking on our door whenever she needs something. Now she just sends a text message."

"How convenient."

Lourdes pulled out a mobile phone, a grey Nokia, and started playing with it.

"I do miss her coming over to the house, but it's for the best," Lourdes said. "Javier's sign language has gotten so sloppy and they were always fighting about it—anyway it was a pain at first to learn how to use this damn thing. You should get one."

"Who would I call?"

"People."

"What people? You're the only one I talk to regularly who has one and I can just call you at home, I mean, why would I want to talk to you if you're not home, if you're out running around or somewhere you can't talk."

On the street an older woman fell, and the sisters watched through the window as two young men helped her up.

"How's Cruz?" Lourdes said.

"Consistent."

"And the children?"

"I don't know."

"What does that mean?"

"I haven't heard from any of them in months. I feel bad."

"They're busy, Vinita, I'm sure they—"

"No, I feel bad that I don't mind."

"Don't mind what?"

"That my children don't call me. You know, I read them all, every mothering book you gave me. I didn't want to be like *her*. I wanted to be a good mother."

"You are a good mother."

"I'm a terrible mother."

"I didn't think you had read any of those books."

"I read some of them, well, parts of them—what are you drinking?"

"Coffee."

"What kind?! I can smell it from here."

"Something from Costa Rica, I think." Lourdes held her cup under Vinita's nose.

"It's potent...nice," Vinita said. "Remind me to buy a pound before we leave—anyway look at me now."

"You look good."

"I look fat."

"You're not fat. *That* woman is fat." Lourdes gestured towards a large woman outside the window.

"And I've become one of those mothers," Vinita said.

"What mothers?"

"The ones whose children never call them."

"Stop."

"I have. I've officially become our mother."

"Please stop. They'll call you."

"Oh the hell with them," Vinita said, waving her hand angrily at the air as if slapping a child who had talked back to her. "I'm exhausted anyway. I have *nothing* else to give them. You were smart Lourdes."

"How so?"

"You stopped after one kid. Good for you."

Lourdes and Javier had one child, a deaf girl. When she was born, they discovered quickly that raising a special needs child felt as if they were raising triplets, each one demanding something different at the exact moment, all day, every day. Neither one ever brought up the subject of having another child. One was enough if they were going to continue teaching and have lives, and Lourdes was about to explain this—again—to Vinita but instead she said, "You're in a mood. Sounds like you're ready to take off again. Like any day now you'll be packing your blue suitcase."

"It's been packed."

Vinita looked out the window, distracted.

"Will you be hiding out locally or heading to L.A.?" Lourdes said. She stood up and put on her coat. "Vinita?"

Vinita looked at Lourdes as though she had not seen her in a while and said, "Where are you going?"

"I have to get to my first class."

"Your *class*...?"

"Oh god don't start this again—"

"Lourdes, you're older than I am. Retire already."

"And do what? Be bored out of my mind like Javier?"

"Travel."

"Javier hates flying. He doesn't even like being in a car anymore."

"Then go by yourself somewhere."

"You can stop now. C'mon. Walk me to my class."

Vinita shook her head. One hand clung to her coffee cup, the other reached out and grabbed Lourdes' hand. They stared at each other.

"Stay home," Lourdes said.

Vinita pulled her sister's hand to her lips and kissed it. She then watched Lourdes through the window. Watched her cross the street and vanish in the crowd, leaving Vinita with the urge to applaud as if she had just witnessed magic sitting in a tent on the Santa Monica Pier. The rain stopped. Umbrellas began to close, one by one, at first, then in unison until they all vanished, and Vinita felt a little more alive when she saw it—a sliver of sunlight on the street, slowly growing wider.

# 6

For twenty minutes Luis complains about the heat and humidity and my broken A/C, and when I ask him *why did you wear jeans, why didn't you wear shorts,* he says, "Because I didn't want to spend my birthday peeling my skin off of these goddamn leather seats that hurt when you slide across them because the cracked leather feels like sandpaper on your skin and you're not helping by covering these holes with tape, because every time your ass slides over the tape, the edges roll up and the heat melts the adhesive and mixes with your sweat and now we got something close to cement and good luck trying to get up and out of this fucking car that belongs in a junkyard—there's Mami! Speed up!"

This is the fourth time in the last hour that Luis is convinced he sees Vinita. From the back every attractive older woman with a good figure and dark hair looks like his mother to him. And for a second she does, and I speed up with hope in my heart only to have the woman turn around and confirm it's not Vinita. Luis sighs each time then starts rambling about nonsense. I turn on the radio. He talks louder. I raise the volume. He talks louder. I give up and turn off the radio, and now he's rambling about dead people and I'm tuning him in and out because he doesn't have an off switch.

"...and the body was on the table, some man, and I was putting cufflinks on him, lion's heads, I think they were, made of gold or maybe they were just painted gold. I must've been seven or eight, and at one point, I drop a cufflink and it rolls under the table so I drop to the floor, crawl all over, looking for the cufflink, and I find it and I crawl out from under the table and stand up and the body, this man, is sitting up, his eyes open now, looking at me, and he's shaking his head and he starts showing me things then dropping them on the floor. A fish, a small globe, a glass vase with blue water that smashes to pieces when it hits the ground, and I look over at Olivia and Ivonne holding ties of different colors and patterns, trying to decide on a tie because this man needed a tie. They're arguing about ties while standing in blue water and that's when you showed up—there's Andres and Rosie."

A man and woman, young, attractive, step into the crosswalk. Luis sinks in his seat until he is completely out of sight.

"Are they gone?" Luis says.

"Are these people you owe money to, people you dated, people you—?"

"All of the above. Are they gone?"

The couple is out of the crosswalk and long gone, but I tell Luis they're walking quickly on the sidewalk along my Granada and for him to stay down and be quiet. This gives me a break from his rambling for about fifteen minutes.

Sometime later Luis is sitting up on his seat again. He turns on the radio. Complains about today's music then shuts off the radio.

"How's the company doing?" Luis asks.

"Fine."

"Have you given any more thought to selling it?"

"I'm not giving you any more money."

"That's not why I'm asking."

Distracted, I turn left when I want to go right. Now we're on Southern Boulevard driving along the Botanical Garden.

"It's time for you to retire, Papi, and keep a closer eye on Mami so we don't have to do this."

"Do what?"

"This driving around the Bronx every time she's had it with her life, with you—"

"Get your feet off the dashboard!"

Luis gets his feet off the dashboard.

"It's Saturday," he says. "It's my birthday. There are other things I'd rather be doing— oh look the Bronx Zoo. Where you all abandoned me and the deaf girl when we were about seven I think it was—that has to be Mami on the corner. Speed up!"

Luis leans his head out the window and opens his mouth then closes it when a woman who is not his mother turns around. He sighs.

# 7

A deaf girl is standing in a barn in front of Picasso's *Guernica*, a mural in desolate tones of black, grey, and white, neither realistic or romantic. A collage of chaos evoking the horrors of war:

grieving woman holding a dead baby

gored horse falling in agony

wounded civilians

a black bull watching

its tail forming a flame

and so on

*Guernica* falls.

When it hits the barn floor, it smashes into tiny pieces and Picasso's figures spill into the barn.

More chaos.

The deaf girl screams.

The grieving woman shakes the dead baby, kisses it, then shakes it again, whispering *wake up wake up*.

The gored horse breaks into a furious gallop, trampling over pieces of the Picasso that roll and turn into diamonds, sparkle and blaze like the northern lights then—*poof*—vanish as the black bull runs in circles, its flaming tail setting everything on fire.

Soon there is too much smoke.

Civilians are dying.

The deaf girl can't breathe.

She runs and runs, runs until she's out of the burning barn, runs until she's on a subway platform in the Bronx, chasing a train as if there won't be any more trains after this one and if she misses it, she'll be screwed, trapped underground with strangers moving in herds, peering down dark tunnels, waiting for trains that will never come.

# 8

The deaf girl was seventeen the first time she saw the painting; a mediocre replica of Picasso's *Guernica* while on a family vacation in Puerto Rico. It was in a 24" x 36" wooden frame, this painting, the frame chipped, the glass scratched, hanging in her grandmother Dolores' sitting room. Standing in front of the painting, the deaf girl asked her grandmother why she kept such a sad piece of art in her home. Dolores moved and stood next to her granddaughter. They stared at the painting for some time then began to sign.

*nothing sad about guernica*
*war sad abuela*
*painting is not about war*
*looks like war*
*it is about marriage*

Dolores walked away. The deaf girl stared at *Guernica* for the rest of her vacation. At the end of the summer, her grandmother gave the deaf girl the painting. It was time, Dolores said, to get rid it, this last thing that belonged to her dead husband.

The deaf girl thinks about *Guernica* as she jumps now on the downtown D train at Kingsbridge Road in the Bronx. One hand clings to her bag, the other to a metal pole, balancing herself on four-inch stilettos. She is cold. But she leaves her coat unbuttoned, revealing a tight black dress with a triangle cutout, baring ample cleavage that lets you know she goes to the gym more than twice a week. Her pocket vibrates. A text message from her mother Lourdes. *Lunch Sunday?* Though the deaf girl has no plans Sunday, she declines. A man smiles and offers his seat. She shakes her head and remains standing even though her feet hurt. When she rides the train, she likes to stand, to feel, on the soles of her feet, its power as the train accelerates, rumbles, shaking her to the core. She shifts her bag from one shoulder to the other, briefly touching her right ear, making sure her hearing aid is still hidden behind hair. Then, like every morning, her eyes scan the train for him, the love of her life. She doesn't search for a handsome man but one with a kind face, approachable, with soft hands like the Cuban she flirted with on the train for weeks, the one she dated for about twenty minutes under a staircase at the end of a subway platform last week. He kissed and licked her all over like a German Shepherd she once knew except the German Shepherd had better breath, she thought. By the time she emerged from the staircase to catch her train, it was over for her. It was only later she realized she didn't even use her deaf voice that always sounded as if she had a sore throat. There was no need to. He never said a word either, never even knew she was deaf.

Right in the heart of the Diamond District, near the corner of 47th and 6th, the deaf girl searches for coffee while standing in front of a Starbucks. She sees the Starbucks but contemplates buying coffee down the street at the Korean place where the coffee is as weak and pale as their tea. A fact that makes her face collapse now into a scowl. She looks through the Starbucks window, at the long coffee line, her left hand a fist, clutching a piece of paper with her coffee order scribbled on it. She bites her lip, shifting her weight from one stiletto to the other, debating, *go in, not go in.* But she used to go into Starbucks all the time until a friend told her he was at a Starbucks on Astor Place at some event for the deaf and the Starbucks employees stared at them when they signed, complained that they weren't buying enough coffee or food, and finally told the deaf group not to come back while hearing patrons were allowed to linger at tables forever and *Are you fucking kidding me* she had signed to her friend, her hands signing the words with such speed and fury that if he had stepped in their path, her long avocado nails would've sliced him in half. Her rage was still with her when, a month later, she read in *The New York Times* that the deaf group was suing Starbucks for discrimination. She hasn't been inside a Starbucks since.

But this morning she wants to go into Starbucks so bad she's ready to cry but crying over coffee, she thinks, is a waste of time when there are so many other things, important things, she has to cry about. She puts her coffee order in her pocket and heads to the Korean place.

The deaf girl arrives at work two minutes early, sipping on Korean coffee. Her boss appears, looks at his watch and gives her a thumbs up. Her expression changes into something like *get away from me* and she moves on as it appears, a memory of him, of them, in his office last month, late at night. An embrace, a kiss, the certainty that this man with soft hands and a face both handsome and kind was indeed *the one*. They made love in the tight space between his file cabinet and bookcase. He handled her body as if it were made of glass, so gentle to the point that she almost fell sleep, her head buried in his shoulder the whole time, random thoughts flashing like subtitles, *bad girl, bad novela, definitely not the one*.

Twenty years ago, instructors at a special school for the deaf threw a party for the deaf girl's eighteenth birthday. She was about to graduate with no plans for college, simply wanted to work, to be independent, get out from under her parents. At the party, a school counselor handed her a gift: a signed document from a company in the Diamond District guaranteeing her a job as a diamond sorter. She liked what she read: *No interview required, no experience necessary, will train.* Per your request, the counselor added, you wouldn't have to engage with anyone. Two months later she was done with her training. An expert with her loupe magnifier, telling everyone she knew that the word *diamond* came from the Greek word *adamas* and how she loved that word and what it meant: unbreakable.

Now the deaf girl sits all day with a loupe magnifier jammed in her eye, inspecting diamonds, sorting the good ones from the bad. Hours of wearing the magnifier used to give her headaches. Now it just gives her nightmares. The other night she dreamt she was looking through her loupe and the stones began to move, like diamond spiders, growing with each step they took, eventually turning on her, eating her alive, loupe and all.

The nightmares have become more frequent, more bizarre.

Last week she dreamt the diamonds had turned into the faces of all the men in her life, past and present. After careful inspection, she found flaws in all of them, every single one landing on the reject pile with the exception of her father, a workaholic who compensated by being extremely generous with his checkbook, by never saying no to the deaf girl. Two nights ago, the diamonds turned into her cousin Luis' face, his features exaggerated, doing what he's done all her life, griping about *everything*: dust he can't reach, the color of his neighbor's walls, mold in his bathroom, his girlfriend, the co-workers he can't stand. Then the diamonds rolled and Luis' face morphed into her grandmother's, speaking about dead children, all boys, all miscarriages, each one named, given a proper burial, even a headstone. The diamonds rolled again, the faces disappeared.

The deaf girl removes the loupe and rubs her eyes, thinking about a horse, if she should get one, a real one, or just a picture of one and where in the hell would she keep a horse in the Bronx. Her stomach growls. She takes her lunch late to ensure the break room is empty so she can sign, in private, with the only other deaf person at work, another transport from the deaf school, a tall, heavy boy. On her way to the break room, she passes a wall of framed company ads, mostly close-ups of diamond rings with tag lines that make her cringe. Her favorite ads are the ones with The Blonde Woman who has it all: perfect skin, small waist, diamond on her finger, a handsome man looking on. If she looks at these ads for more than five seconds, she falls into a black hole that takes her days to climb out of. She walks quickly by the ads and sticks her head in the break room to find two men in deep conversation over sandwiches. They look at her and smile. One of them pulls out a chair for her. The deaf girl turns and walks away.

She chews on a protein bar in an empty stairwell next to the deaf boy. He bites into his protein bar and makes a face. He'd rather be eating a pizza, but she convinced him, months ago, that protein bars will take him from fat to fit in no time, a crock of shit he believed until he lost three pounds in a week. He hates eating in the cold stairwell and argues for their return to the warm break room, trying to convince her no one cares they are deaf. But she's positive they're making fun of their signing and he drops the argument. They eat in silence for a few minutes. He starts signing about a favorite TV show, did she watch it last night. Before she can answer, he notices she looks more exhausted than usual and he signs.

*your eyes are red*
*no sleep*
*sorry*
*bad dreams*
*about*
*guernica fell*
*where*
*in the barn*
*was there fire*
*lots*
*did you burn again*

A door opens. A draft caresses their necks. She stops signing.

A co-worker, a young man, steps between them, smiles at them, then down the stairwell he goes. They continue eating with a soundtrack barely audible through their hearing aids: heavy steps descending, echoing, fading; another door opening, closing, loudly, its vibrations shooting through the metal railings and steps, tickling the soles of their feet. They extend their necks over the railing and peer down the stairwell. They wait for more vibrations. Nothing. A Diet Coke spills. She jumps up trying to rescue her stilettos from the splash but slips and collapses on him. They laugh and a memory steps in and takes her away, and she's sitting on her grandmother's porch in Puerto Rico, her best friend at her side; a ten-year-old deaf girl from down the street that made her laugh. The deaf girls were always outside in the sun until one day some neighborhood boys started mocking their sign language by waving their hands wildly in front of them like mad men, laughing the whole time. After that the deaf girl and her friend would hide in the barn, away from the sun and the boys, their little hands fluttering in the air, baby chicks pecking at their feet.

# 9

.

Summers are getting hotter in the Bronx. More humid. I say
this to myself as I stand on the side of the Granada, pumping it
with gas. Luis thinks I was talking to him. He starts rambling
in the front seat about climate change. Greenhouse gases. I
don't know what he's talking about. Quickly he gets bored. Then silent.

Luis opens and closes the glove box. He repeats this. With the
back of his hand, he wipes sweat off his forehead. Looks around the
car. Fidgets.

As a boy Luis was content wherever he was. Just give him a toy, ball,
chalk, etc. He was happy.

Now it's the opposite. No matter where he is, he wants to be somewhere else. Like right now he's climbing over the front seat and sits in
the back seat. He looks out the window. By the time I'm done pumping gas, he's asleep. When I get in the car and slam the door closed, he
opens his eyes for a second.

I own a dressmaking business and the building it's housed in. Been
married for forty-five years. Raised three children. Never played fa-
vorites with them. Paid for whatever they needed growing up. Food,

clothes, college educations, weddings. I was a good father, I think.

Until I'm around Luis.

I had high hopes for Luis when he went to college right after high school for a degree in Environmental Science. He was obsessed for a while with climate change and the demise of Earth. Then a year into the program, he announced to Vinita and I that spending his days thinking about the end of the world was too much for him. He dropped out.

After that Luis developed a living-in-the-moment attitude. He never makes plans. Or sets goals. He's the only one of my children who has never been married. Though there have been many girlfriends. And boyfriends. Of all shapes, sizes and colors. He doesn't discriminate. He says he's attracted to who he's attracted to. The longest he's lived with anyone is two years. A guy named Angelo who came from money. A handsome Italian with blue eyes who wore the nicest clothes. Very pricey stuff he shared with Luis since they wore the same size. Had the same haircut. Went to the same gym. Shared the same bed, but you would never know it the way they behaved in public. Never a display of affection between them. Instead they were always clowning around, playing pranks, looking for trouble like buddies or brothers. Still I was sure Luis was in love with him until Ivonne told me he wasn't. Luis just loved doubling his wardrobe, she said. When they broke up and Angelo moved out, I went over to comfort Luis. He was in tears. He tried to make a joke of it. Said he wasn't crying because Angelo left but because he had taken his clothes with him. But I didn't believe him. Ivonne told me later they broke up because they wanted different things and said nothing more. I suspect Angelo wanted a lover and Luis wanted the brother he never had.

And then there's Ginger.

Though they've lived together briefly here and there, Ginger has been Luis' longest relationship. Four years on and off. A receptionist at a hair salon. An Irish girl with a knockout figure who drinks like every day is St. Patrick's Day. Luis hasn't mentioned the latest awful thing she's done to him so they must be off this week.

As for work, Luis' only requirement is that the job has to be fun. Once it stops being fun, he moves on. Depends on me to carry him until he lines up his next gig. I always say I'm not lending him money, but I always do. Not because I want to help him. Because I want to ease my guilt for failing him. After all he was the boy I was responsible for. Vinita oversaw the girls who have their flaws but are miles ahead of Luis. I don't know what I did wrong with him. But I fucked up somewhere.

I put on my seat belt. On the front seat I see Vinita's picture. I pick it up. It's a photo Lourdes took last year. We were at a restaurant celebrating something. Vinita is wearing a blue dress. Like always, she looks beautiful. We're both sixty-seven. Yet Vinita looks more than twenty years younger than me thanks to years of facials, face creams, diets, soaking her face in bowls of ice.

When she dyes the grey out of her hair, I have her do the same to mine. My desperate attempt to keep looking like her husband instead of her father.

I turn on the car. Luis opens his eyes. He stretches. He yawns.

"Puerto Rico," he says. "I can't remember the last time I was there."

I pull out of the gas station, edge the Granada to the curb. Check for traffic.

"I want to see *Abuela*. I miss her dogs. I miss walking the coffee fields."

I pull out into traffic.

"I'm going to Puerto Rico next week."

"Don't you have to work, Luis?"

Luis waves me off. Like I had just reminded him he had a dentist appointment next week. One he could easily cancel.

"You should come with, Papi."

# 10

His mother's curlers were never to be touched, the boy knew this, he knew it was a bad thing, like talking in church or swearing or crossing on a red light. They were made of hard plastic, these curlers, with holes on the side so the air could circulate, allowing the hair to dry quickly, evenly. It always amazed Vinita, even after years of use, how something so simple, so ordinary, could add so much volume to her hair, could take it from one extreme (dull, lifeless) to another (smooth, silky). She guarded these colored tubes—pastels mostly—like they were diamonds or rare coins, again, never to be touched.

Yet there he was, little Luis Santana, shoving blue clay into a pink curler, quietly, in a closet among brooms and mops and a Hoover vacuum; its hose a snake a moment ago, then a friend, now a mother to the blue worms that poured from the pink tube. The boy was on his knees, sweating, his Buster Browns cushioning him, the heels digging into his khaki shorts, drawing horseshoes on his buttocks. It was cramped in this closet. Plastic bottles everywhere. Some with handles that the boy had assembled into a semi-circle. The taller ones standing watch like guards in a castle, there to protect him: the cantankerous *Ammonia*; his less volatile brother *Clorox*; the sweet-tempered *Downy*; their leader *Mr. Clean*, the bald man who always mocked his mother with his arms crossed, his eyebrows arched. All of them releasing fumes that were now harassing Luis, forcing him to stretch his T-shirt over his nose like a bandit. It was dark in this closet except for the ivory band that glowed and gushed from his father's flashlight on the floor; a silvery thing that looked as if it had fallen off some machine, a robot perhaps, like the one Luis admires on *Lost in Space*. He squinted in the dim light and shoved more clay into the curler until they poured into his hand, these clay worms, babies he delivered to their Hoover mother laying them snugly in the accordion groves on her back. He studied the hose covered in blue clay, his mouth moving, slowly chewing on his last piece of strawberry taffy. Chewing until the taffy was small and flat like the communion wafer he tasted for the first time at his holy Communion last Sunday; a thin white wafer that tasted like paper then got stuck on the roof of his mouth for ten minutes.

Luis swallowed the strawberry taffy. His lower lip moved up over the top one and he blew air, a strawberry-scented breeze that gently ruffled the dark bangs against his forehead.

On the other side of the closet door, Celia Cruz was singing "Sueños de Luna." Her voice streaming from speakers on a phonograph encased in a mahogany console with a center compartment that held liquor. Luis bobbed his head to the music until the cracks on the closet door began to leak with the aroma of *sofrito*, a blend of herbs, onions, garlic, peppers and coriander that Vinita used to give a bright yellow color to her rice. His mother's voice wailed with off-key attempts to sing along with Celia. She was content, Luis thought, so much so that nothing bothered her now. Luis knew his mother was happiest when she had the place to herself. He learned quickly to stay out of her way. To hide and play inside closets, under beds or wherever he could fit. Unlike his sisters, he was still too young to be outside alone, a thought that annoyed Luis now, prompting him to squeeze the clay worms in his hands, then mold them into a blue golf ball.

The closet door opened.

And there was Vinita in a robe. Her mouth open, staring at her curler, unsure if it was pink or blue. She crossed her arms, raised an eyebrow. Never said a word. Not even when she stood over the kitchen sink scrubbing the curler, frantically, as if the curler had a really bad itch; or when she discovered the dirty horseshoes on Luis' shorts, convinced she had already wiped them away with a kitchen towel that morning or yesterday or the day before. With a hand, she wiped away the horseshoes and banished her son to the living room, the Santana Bay, they called it, which Luis now entered slowly, where every piece of furniture, every vase, every knick-knack had its own warning, its own story etched on little white cards that lived in Luis' head. The card in front him now read: *Do Not Touch. Coffee Table. Built in 1941 in Puerto Rico by Grandpa Santana from a ceiba tree that fell over in a storm.*

When Luis walked through the Santana Bay, he kept his arms folded across his chest to keep them from knocking something over or leaving a fingerprint where a fingerprint shouldn't be. Luis restricted himself to the sofa, a walnut frame with lime green cushions peppered with lemon drops, preserved in plastic that crinkled and popped as Luis sat on it. He closed his eyes and swayed on the plastic, making it sing, pretending he was trapped in a giant Jiffy Pop container. It was here where Luis and his family gathered, in this room dominated by three large windows, their glossy white moldings framing Puerto Rico's San Juan Bay painted on shades that were now pulled down. A painted ocean dominated the center shade while the sun peaked through the one on its right; the left shade provided a view of El Morro, "a sixteenth-century fortress built to protect the town from attack by sea," Luis would recite like a tourist guide whenever someone visited. "It's made of stones with towers and tunnels and prisons and parrots—"

"Barracks, Luis, barracks," his father would say.

Luis sat there staring at the ocean, at the waves that never moved, the sun that never set. Vinita entered the room with a bowl of pomegranate seeds in one hand and sat on the other side of the sofa. Food was not allowed in the Santana Bay and Luis opened his mouth to remind her but instead got up from the sofa, turned on the television then moved to a chair, also in plastic, on the other side of the room.

He sat there and watched Vinita watch an old movie. If someone were to peer through a window now—or any day of the week—they would probably mistake Vinita for a neighbor or babysitter, definitely not his mother. She treated Luis with the kind of indifference women save for salesmen and bill collectors, not for their sons. She was never mean or rude to the boy. She simply tolerated him the way one puts up with a repairman, because you have too, not because you want to. She doesn't want to be this way, she explained to her sister once, but she can't help it. She taught her daughters early on how to depend on each other instead of their mother. Olivia and Ivonne knew how to feed themselves by the time they were five, how to pull up and mount chairs to reach cabinets filled with glasses and dishware and food and all sorts of snacks. Luis hasn't caught on yet despite her efforts. She's not sure if it's because he's not bright or if he just wants to be taken care of. Her daughters are self-sufficient now, but as toddlers, they were demanding, exhausting. By the time Luis was born, apathy had already moved in and settled on her like dust.

Vinita stood up and removed her robe, revealing a fitted blue dress. She removed her slippers and stepped into a pair of three-inch black pumps that waited for her on one side of the sofa. No matter what time of day it was Vinita was often dressed as if she were the leading lady in one of the old movies she watched. For years Vinita would tell anyone who'd listen—in vivid details—that in her youth she lived in Hollywood, appeared as an extra in films at Warner Bros., made a screen test, and was even offered a contract as a studio player but it fell through. However, the details of the end of her dream to be a movie star were not vivid but rather vague. For years, whenever an old Warner Bros. film with a crowd scene was on television, Vinita would insist she was there. Her Hollywood stories reminded the family of the stories Vinita had brought from Puerto Rico in her youth. The ones about how Vinita, as a teen, had won an island beauty pageant when in reality she had been the third runner-up. Or how a foreign prince once visited her family's coffee plantation, fell in love with her and asked her to marry him, but she said *no* when in reality it was a neighbor's daughter the prince had proposed to. There are many stories Vinita still repeats with vivid details. *If you're going to lie,* she would tell her children, *don't be vague, be specific,* like if you show up to school without your homework, don't just say your dog ate your homework, say your red-and-white Welsh Corgi with a limp ate your homework. If not, they'll see right through you.

Luis watched Vinita settle on the sofa. Her movie (Hitchcock's *To Catch a Thief*) had already started, but it didn't matter for she had seen it many times. She stuck out her tongue and placed a pomegranate seed carefully on it so as not to disturb her lipstick. Her eyes never left the television screen. Whatever Grace Kelly would say, Vinita would repeat, sometimes two, three times. Grace now sat in a car, then was gently forced into a horizontal position by Cary Grant as he leaned in for a kiss. The screen went black. A commercial. The cue Luis was waiting for. He began to ramble about this and that. Vinita's eyes spun in her head.

"Go," she said. "Leave the door open and stay in the stairwell."

The Santanas resided near the Bronx Zoo where the lions, even the gorillas, got along better than Luis and his sisters. They lived in a pre-war building, a grey brick structure with a stairwell that served as a playground for Luis; each step made of marble as pale as a corpse, their dark veins flowing with black blood. Luis hopped in between the veins now while he balanced himself on the iron railing coated with layers of peeling paint that betrayed colors from years past. The stairwell walls were the color of wet sand. They provided a canvas for the boy's drawings, created with chalk of various colors he had taken from his second-grade classroom at his Catholic school, then obliterated with a stolen eraser from the same classroom. It was in this stairwell, alone, that Luis was the most content. Standing for hours at the landing window. Mesmerized by everything. Black-and-white pigeons flying in circles against grey skies like a scene from one of his mother's old movies. Listening to traffic. Peering through metal rails at the free children below. Drawing on the walls. Watching chalk dust float into the air then linger in a shaft of light.

## II

Ivonne wanders a farm in a nightgown. The sun is out.

She arrives at a horse stable. A wooden structure painted blue with a tin roof. The sliding barn door is open. Just inside she sees a dozen or so children, mostly boys, in shorts and T-shirts of various colors.

She does not know who these children are.

They are completely still.

As if posing for a picture.

Standing together yet apart.

Ivonne goes inside the stable.

Everything is as it was yesterday.

Except there are three black trunks, closed, in the middle of the stable.

And someone has drawn a red line on the floor. Going from one stall on the left to the other one on the right. The children stand near the red line but not past it.

Ivonne moves between the children. Studies their faces but there is nothing there.

No excitement.

Or anxiety.

Or confusion.

Nothing.

At the other end of the stable, the sliding barn door starts to open.

A man appears in a white shirt.

The children finally move.

They inch closer to the red line but do not pass it.

The man says, Who wants to make a quarter?

The children raise their hands.

The man says, On the count of three.

Ivonne moves to the side.

One...two...three.

The children run to the black trunks and open them.

One trunk has men's clothing.

One has women's clothing.

One has shoes for men and women.

As if they had all the time in the world, the children dig through the trunks.

They pull out shirts or pants or dresses or shoes.

They hold these items up, examine them, toss them back in the trunks, pull out more items and repeat the process again and again. When they find items they are satisfied with, they carry them into the horse stalls in silence.

Ivonne moves to the first stall. The horse that stood there yesterday is gone. In its place is a male corpse lying on a gurney. There are three children working to dress the corpse.

One is buttoning a shirt.

Another zipping the pants.

Another slipping on shoes.

This scene is repeated for Ivonne when she goes to the next stall and the next one and the next one, except sometimes it is a female corpse and the children are maneuvering a dress instead of a shirt and pants.

Ivonne goes up to a little girl digging into a trunk and says, Where are my horses?

The girl smiles, shrugs and disappears into a stall with a blue dress.

Ivonne looks at the man in the white shirt, and before she can say anything, he shrugs. Ivonne exits the stable.

She wanders the farm searching for her horses.

It begins to rain.

# 12

was born Ivonne Milagros Santana forty-three years ago. My last name has changed often. I've been married five times, I'm told, but some days I can only remember four marriages. Today is one of those days. It's hard for me to be married. It's hard for me not to be married. My mother Vinita says it's because I'm afraid to be alone with my thoughts. That I need to be around people or noise. As a child, she says, my sister and brother were happy to be off on their own in a quiet place, but I always had to attach myself to someone. Or be constantly talking. Always trying to save dying conversations because the silence that followed was too much for me so I'd turn on a radio or television or open a window to let in the sound of traffic. I don't remember being that way as a child.

My family and friends in the Bronx talk about me a lot and not behind my back which I prefer, no, they do it to my face, often accusing me of awful things like shopping for husbands like I shop for clothes. Never trying anything on to make sure it fits. If it looks good on the hanger, I buy it, they say, and hope for the best, and when I finally accept that something doesn't fit right, that it isn't going to work out, the return window has closed and I'm stuck with it and that's when lawyers get involved, settlements are negotiated, and you go back to your maiden name and swear you'll never change it again. And they say because I marry wealthy men and marry quickly, that love doesn't play a role in the *arrangement*, as they call it. Over the years, they have given me many nicknames:

*puta de dinero* (money whore)
*parásito codicioso* (greedy parasite)
*bruja rica* (rich witch)
*buscadora de oro sucia* (dirty gold digger)

And these nicknames are said with a smile, meant as a joke, and I laugh, but they bother me because I'm not thinking *Those names aren't true.* I'm thinking *Those names are a little true.*

Now I live on a farm in Ohio. Almost twenty acres in the middle of nowhere. In a town so dreary, so inconsequential that I refuse to say its name. There are horses and blueberries and sweet corn that we need to attend to, and by we, I mean a few workers that come and go during the week. On the weekends, Ben (husband number five) likes to do the chores, likes to be outdoors getting his hands dirty, enjoying the fresh air. I don't do chores. I sometimes go outside and do things, but lately I sit around watching the soap operas I became addicted to in college, still in awe at how characters don't age, how some stay married forever.

After graduating with a degree in business administration, I set out to own a business. I wanted to build wealth. I got an office job at a big corporation to see how the place ran. The CEO flirted with me for weeks. He was handsome. Married. One thing led to another, and before I knew it, we were characters in a bad soap opera doing bad things. He left his wife, asked me to marry him. He owned an apartment in the city. A house in Connecticut. He had a six- figure salary (not including bonuses) and I figured I didn't need to own a business to build my wealth, my god, here it is right in front of me. I wasn't in love or anything close to it, but I said *yes*. I was twenty-one. By time I was twenty-six, I had a four-year-old son named Raul, was a kept housewife, twenty-five pounds overweight and miserable until one day the CEO came home and told me it was over, and I was relieved, ecstatic. He was in love with a waitress but not to worry, my son and I were going to be taken care of. And as he said that, I felt myself leave my body and float to the ceiling, and I looked down and wasn't sure if I was looking at my life or a scene from a soap opera that had grown so predictable I had figured out the ending months ago.

He left me the house, which I sold and bought another one in the Bronx near my family. I lost the weight, reinvented myself and started over, and the rest of my marriages played out the same way. Except my third one with Gerald. He was like a sweater that didn't fit at first, then, just as I was starting to grow into it, into him, he was gone. Killed in a car accident in the Bronx.

Gerald.

The nothingness of the town we live in torments me now with the kind of anguish Marlene Dietrich turned into an art form in those old movies my mother turned me on to. The ones that keep me company at night when everyone has gone to bed and the house settles and my heart aches in silence, and I think about how my family in the Bronx never checks in on me anymore. Except for my brother Luis who calls occasionally to ask for money or give me environmental warnings ("Don't let them use pesticides!"). It was not my idea to move to a farm. I was perfectly happy in our Bronx home just steps away from all things family. But Ben was miserable in the city with all its dirty air and noise and way too many people for him. And it was his misery—and my willingness to try anything once—that led us to this farm where we're awoken every day before sunrise by a rooster's crow, a sound more startling than a car alarm going off at 2:00 a.m. outside your bedroom window in the Bronx.

This morning, my son is gone, sitting on a plane on his way back to Puerto Rico to see some guy. The night before he told me, *I think I'm in love*, though there was no excitement in his voice. You would have thought he had just announced, to no one in particular, that he was going for a walk.

I go into the kitchen. I make breakfast. I sit at the table with Ben and the silence. Silence is such a part of our lives that I often find myself setting a place for it at the table. I don't know what bothers me more. That I set a place for it or that no one notices. It wasn't always this way. When we first arrived on the farm, we were all non-stop chatter, excited about exploring a new place like children in a playground they had never been to, filled with horses they had never ridden. Two years later, and the excitement long gone, the chatter stopped and the silence arrived like a flood, pouring through windows and doors, settling in every room. To prove my mother wrong, I don't turn on radios or televisions or open windows anymore.

# 13

At 4:58 p.m., the deaf girl puts her loupe away, freshens her makeup. A train ride later she is at her new gym on the Upper East Side. It's been a few weeks since she joined, yet she hates this gym and their rundown machines. She loved her old gym with their modern machines that helped maintain her tight figure, her small waist. The membership was much more than other gyms, but she didn't mind; it was a serious gym with serious bodybuilders, there to work out, everyone keeping to themselves. Except for the staff member who sold her the membership, no one knew she was deaf. No one bothered her. Then one night two men were checking her out while she was walking to the water fountain. She leaned over for a sip of water when she felt a tap on her shoulder. An old girlfriend from her deaf school days. To her horror, her friend began to sign, right there in front of the men, going on about how great it was to see her, let's work out together sometime, go for coffee, anywhere except Starbucks of course. The girl held up her mobile phone. *How great are these*, she signed, *do you have one, let's exchange numbers*. The deaf girl didn't respond with sign language. She took the girl's mobile phone out of her hand, entered her name and number then went home. The next day the deaf girl joined the new gym where she exercises now in dark glasses and a baseball cap. Even her own mother wouldn't recognize her.

At 8:33 p.m., the deaf girl steps off the D train at Kingsbridge Road. A man passes by her. Their eyes lock briefly. She looks over her shoulder at him. He steps onto the train then turns to her. The train doors close. Through the glass she sees him nod at her. She nods back. Smiles are exchanged. The train pulls out.

She walks through her neighborhood, waving or nodding at neighbors, people who don't even know her name or that she's deaf. She stops in front of her house, the one her parents helped her buy; a small two-story brick house with two steps that lead to a porch. She stands on the porch for a while.

The deaf girl enters the house, greeted by *Guernica* hanging in the foyer.

Then he appears, this man with rough hands and a face that is everything but kind. And it starts as soon as their eyes meet, their *diálogo de sordos* (dialog of the deaf):

*a conversation where each party speaks but no one listens, refusing to hear each other's point of view; a term frequently used in political contexts, i.e., U.S. and Iranian nuclear negotiations are an ongoing dialog of the deaf.*

And because she is deaf and he isn't, and because he knew this when they met and married three years ago, it annoys her that the hearing man still hasn't learned to sign despite the many how-to-sign books in the house. Recently she gave him another book, one geared at children with colorful illustrations of foods and farm animals; a cover promising in cool blue letters that learning sign language would be *Fun and Easy!* Like the others, he refuses to open this book, standing by his defense: "Why should I learn to sign when I can text you."

Their *diálogo de sordos* has caused the deaf girl great stress. Once when her Aunt Vinita visited, the deaf girl's strained face reminded her aunt of her own mother's. Vinita asked her niece repeatedly what was wrong. The deaf girl kept signing over and over that she was *fine*; a scene reenacted when her mother came by a week later, nagging until the deaf girl broke down and confessed how unhappy she was with her husband, her job. And Lourdes, always so economical and resourceful, *Miss Two-for-One*, gave her daughter one solution for both problems: *Don't leave one until you have the next one lined up or you'll regret it.*

The hearing man is carrying on in the foyer. She places her coat on the hooks that hang under *Guernica*, her eyes settling briefly on the grieving woman with the dead baby.

Then she turns to him.

They met three years ago on a blind date a friend of hers had arranged. The hearing man was given instructions to speak slowly so she could read his lips; told never to look away while he was speaking because she would miss a word or two and he'd have to repeat himself. He followed instructions very well that night. She missed a lot of his words but was able to piece things together. He worked in a finance company, in their mail room. And even though she didn't care for his bad jokes ("You sort diamonds, I sort mail, but you win cause rock always beats paper ha ha ha"), she liked the way this Puerto Rican looked. Like Colin Farrell except darker. She would taste him once, she decided that night, then be rid of him.

But the taste was too addictive. For six months, they had sex all over the city. In cabs, stairwells, elevators, the park, empty subway cars. They engaged like boxers, rough and brutal, then off to their own corners they went. After a month, he moved in with her. One night they were sitting around doing their taxes when they realized they'd qualify for a larger standard deduction if they were married. They debated about getting married, casually, as if they were trying to decide which restaurant to go to. A week before taxes were due, they married at City Hall. Only Lourdes and Vinita witnessed the whole thing.

And since then, everything has turned into an argument.

The hearing man paces the foyer in front of the deaf girl. He is yelling about something. She looks at his lips. All she can make out are two words—*beam* and *bedroom*. Her eyes roll.

It had been her idea, the beam, a very bad one, he had told her; this long wooden thing she bought that looked like oak but he had been certain it wasn't. *But there it is on the receipt*, she had said way too loud in her deaf voice, her hands signing the words, but the signs meant nothing to him. She might as well have been swatting a fly and she knew this, but she signed anyway to remind herself who she was. She ignored his objections and hired workmen to install the beam, with him nagging the whole time. *Are there enough screws*, he kept saying, *use lots of screws.* When the workmen were done, he hated the beam. Hated the way it hovered over their bed, threatening to fall on them while they slept. Hated the way it made the room look like a barn, but that was the point, she had signed. And last week, when the beam fell one night near him, she stood there paralyzed, dazzled by all the blood, wishing she had painted the beam the shade of red pouring from his ear while diamonds rolled around him. The next morning she awoke and there he was, snoring away, the beam still up, not a sign of blood or diamonds anywhere.

The deaf girl was relieved, disappointed.

The war of the beam continues, moving now from the foyer to the living room where Maria Callas is tackling an aria in Bellini's *Norma.* The hearing man stops arguing in mid- sentence, closes his eyes and listens, as if he's never heard this opera he plays night after night. He raises the volume. The deaf girl can feel the vibrations coming from the speakers he has set up throughout the house. Callas is digging into "Casta diva" and her coloratura agility is causing him to lose his breath. Sweat is pouring. Baggy pants can't hide his erection now. An unspoken ceasefire is declared, and they mate. She gets lost in the biting, the hair pulling, the vibrations of his deep grunts, her gasps cut short with each brutal thrust, trying to vocalize her pleasure with a voice that isn't there; then he's tossing her up and over and he feels like iron inside her, pounding away until something deep inside her goes off and she shudders, over and over, and it feels like the happiest day of her life plus two more, all strung together.

After the mating, he sleeps. She cuddles him from behind, burying her nose in his back, inhaling the smell of sweat and cheap cologne while Maria Callas spills out of the speaker next to their bed; her voice all passion and rage rattling the window above them, the vibrations shooting through the wall, the headboard, the deaf girl's body, poor thing afraid to sleep, to dream.

She pulls away from him and lies there, her eyes wide open. Moonlight has stolen the color from everything; it's as if she's seeing the room through an old black-and-white television: her red lamp shades look black, her pastel blue walls grey. She looks at the beam, the oak black as tar now. Then she holds her hand up and stares at her wedding ring, the gold band now silver in the moonlight, the small diamond barely visible. She removes the ring and tosses it on the nightstand. It hits the lamp base, rolls then falls on the floor. A sigh. She considers searching for the ring but doesn't.

The next day she informs him the beam is staying up and she doesn't want to discuss it anymore. This pisses him off.

For days they carry on as if the other doesn't exist, preparing their own meals, eating and sleeping in separate rooms; she in the bedroom with her beam, he in the living room with Maria Callas, tonight singing her Violetta in Verdi's *La traviata*, sounding more restrained than usual. Still Callas' emotional collapse at the end of act three rips him apart, and when the deaf girl enters the kitchen with her dirty plate, he is standing over the sink in tears, masturbating.

Undetected, she retreats and stands in the hallway in the dark, touching herself, watching him until he's done, tiptoeing away with her dirty plate as he wipes up his mess with a kitchen towel.

The next morning he lingers in the foyer, half-dressed for work, his shirt unbuttoned. She enters from the bathroom and heads towards her coat hanging under *Guernica*. He stands in her way. Nothing between them except the smell of coffee and Maria Callas finishing up Aida's "Triumphal March." He moves closer and speaks slowly, offering her a truce. A dinner invitation that evening. She accepts with a casual nod, but inside she is aching for him, feels herself surrendering, already coming up with an excuse for her boss as to why she is late.

Then she looks at his rough hands, hanging there, lifeless, and every urge and desire she has vanishes. He moves closer and touches her down there. She smacks his hand away. He shoves her, she shoves back, hard, his body hits the wall, *Guernica* falls, shatters, glass everywhere. Maria Callas is soaring into a high C in "O patria mia" when he slips on broken glass. The deaf girl moves swiftly, straddling him, undoing his pants. He pulls it out, she guides it in, the connection is made.

Sometime later she is at work sorting through diamonds, the loupe in her eye, thinking about him. About his ability to take her breath away, a skill that has always outweighed his defects. The light catches a cluster of diamonds, blinding her for a second. A pause. She focuses on a diamond. One side has a pattern of arrows from the top. She flips it over. Eight hearts in small V-shapes. She wonders what it would be like to have eight hearts. Would you be able to turn off each one at will? If one heart grew cold and died, would the body still function like a car with a taillight out?

# 14

I think he was about five when Luis started seeing dead people no one else could see.

Whenever he saw one at home or outside or at family gatherings, he'd make an announcement. Vinita and I brushed it off as a child playing make-believe. People laughed at his announcements in the beginning. Over time they stopped laughing when Luis' announcements became specific. Instead of just seeing a man in a brown suit, suddenly he was naming relatives of people who had died long ago, years before he was born.

Once we were at Lourdes and Javier's house for a party and they had colleagues there. Luis went up to a professor he had never met and said, "Your Grandmother Amelia says there's nothing wrong with your hallway light."

Vinita and I watched as the professor's mouth dropped open.

Luis added, "The light that's always going on and off. In the hallway. There's nothing wrong with it. So stop changing the lightbulbs. It's just your grandmother saying hello."

The professor's face turned white. Vinita and I grabbed Luis and left the party.

We did nothing for a while until Luis started making announcements at his school and frightening everyone. Children on the playground. Teachers in the classroom. Finally we sat Luis down and told him to ignore these dead people, to say nothing. Telling a boy to ignore a problem was probably, well, *definitely* not the way to deal with this, but it's what we did.

Luis obeyed.

Yet we always knew when he'd see these dead people, because he'd tilt his head, his mouth would open and stay open, his eyes would look up, then forward, then down like he was studying toys on shelves trying to decide which one he wanted. Then he would freeze for a few seconds, close his eyes briefly and look in another direction and he'd be back to normal.

Luis is looking out my windshield now with his head tilted, his mouth open. I park the Granada in front of Van Cortlandt Park. I wait it out. His eyes close. He looks in another direction and says, "When Raul was a kid, I used to bring him here to ride horses. I was a good uncle."

I wipe sweat off my face.

"Did Ivonne ever ask you to bring Raul here?"

"Never," I say. "So what do you got going on next week?"

"Just readings—and Ivonne had the time to bring Raul here but not the interest."

"Readings? Are you a poet now?"

"They're called readings, but no reading goes on. I just interpret signs, deliver messages from loved ones and people cry and blah blah blah and I'm getting busier, but I know how you don't like to hear about that part of my life so I'll shut up...And when I couldn't bring Raul here, Mami would. That's when she started liking this place. Isn't that the bench we found her on like three years ago with her blue suitcase?"

Luis is pointing out the window. The Granada coughs and trembles. She doesn't sound good. Luis shakes his head and says, "We're going to end up fucking walking."

"She just needs a tune-up."

I turn off the engine.

"With all your money, I don't understand why you're still driving this pile of shit."

"Why don't you sit here and I'll go look for your mother."

Luis gets out of the car with Vinita's picture. He slams the door and he doesn't just use his hand. He throws his whole body into it like he did as a kid at the end of a tantrum or the beginning of one.

"You didn't slam it hard enough," I say.

"Best fucking birthday ever."

"Bring me back something to drink."

"Sure. I'll see if I can find you a new car too."

"Need some money?"

"Fuck you."

"Make sure it's cold!"

He gives me the finger.

He's a good kid.

# 15

Red chalk. The boy was holding it in his little hand when his mother came looking for him.

"Luis?"

He turned from the stairwell window, walked up the stairs then stopped when he saw Vinita standing in the apartment doorway. He looked at her without saying a word. The boy knew she didn't want anything except confirmation that he was there, that he hadn't wandered off. They locked eyes for a moment, then Vinita glanced at her watch. She started to turn back into the apartment when something caught her eye. She stepped into the hallway and looked at the wall. Her eyes roamed over Luis' drawing, startling the boy for his mother had never stopped to look at his chalk creations. Luis could remember her pausing in front of them to adjust her stockings or drop something into her purse, moments that were brief, rare, but look at her now, studying this chalk drawing of something that resembled a white tree with red balls.

"Balls don't grow on trees," she said.

"They're not balls, Mami, they're apples."

"Apples?"

Vinita studied the drawing some more.

"Apples aren't that round, Luis, at least not the Red Delicious ones we buy, maybe the Honeycrisp, but those are too sweet for your father so we don't buy those. The Red Delicious are wider at the top and narrow at the bottom, and when you turn them upside down, they have four rounded stumps and look like, like the teeth in the back of your mouth—where did you get the red chalk?"

Luis thought about the day his teacher, a nun, dropped the red chalk in his classroom. On her way to pick it up, she unintentionally kicked it under a bookcase. She made a face, picked up another piece of chalk from the chalk holder and continued with her lesson. At the end of class, as everyone was filing out, Luis purposedly dropped a pencil and kicked it under the bookcase. He got on his knees and retrieved the items. The pencil went behind his ear, the red chalk in his pocket.

"Luis, where did you get the red chalk from?"

The boy was standing in front of a vending machine now; it wasn't filled with soda or candy but an assortment of lies, and after a quick scan of his choices, the boy made his selection. "I found it in the laundry place." And because her face told him she wasn't convinced, Luis added, "Behind a silver machine." More details, he thought. "With a dent on the side."

Vinita was about to say something, something she had heard in church, he was sure of it. But when dramatic music poured out of her television and filled the stairwell, Vinita ran inside as if she had left something burning on the stove.

Luis looked at his drawing.

*Apples aren't that round.*

He picked up his eraser and proceeded to erase his apples. He was still erasing when his father came up the stairs carrying dresses on hangers covered in plastic.

"Papi!"

Cruz bent over and swooped up Luis with his free arm. He kissed the boy's forehead and said, "Hey, little hombre."

"Did you make those dresses?"

"I don't make dresses anymore. I have workers do that now. Where's your mother?"

"Watching Grace Jelly."

Cruz giggled. "*Kelly*, Grace *Kelly*."

He set Luis back on the ground and went inside the apartment as the Italians from next door came up the stairs carrying grocery bags, talking in their native language.

"Did you buy any apples?" Luis said.

The Italians continued their conversation while they looked in their brown paper bags. A few seconds later they were gone, and Luis had a peach in his hand. He went to the stairwell window, shoved his hand between the safety bars and dropped the peach into the alley below.

He went up to the door opposite their apartment and banged on it. He waited. He banged again and the door opened. Mrs. Rivera appeared, looking as though she had tumbled out of *Hansel and Gretel* with her long, odd-shaped nails, two layers of coats, soiled and tattered, that she never took off, not even in the summertime, coats that her dead husband had bought for her. And though she looked slovenly, she smelled like bread right out of the oven. She always did and Luis liked this about her. Her apartment behind her was dark. The light in the stairwell was causing Mrs. Rivera to squint. She didn't say a word, just looked at the boy as if he were some farm animal, a pony, roaming free in her stairwell and would someone please put him back in his stall.

"Mrs. Rivera, do you have any apples?"

She looked right through him, took a step back and slammed her door.

Luis turned around and went inside. He peeked into the Santana Bay. Vinita was still watching her movie in silence until she repeated a Grace Kelly line. He entered the kitchen and found his father at the kitchen table eating while he read the newspaper. Luis stared at a wooden bowl in the center of the kitchen table filled with plastic fruit. A pear. Rubbery grapes. Bananas that were too yellow. But no apples.

Luis went to the kitchen counter and stood on his toes reaching for a handful of *platanos*: green bananas, thinly sliced, then fried, now cold. He was nibbling on his last one when he saw it at the other end of the counter: another bowl, a simple one with no history, no warnings, filled with fruit, real fruit: mangos, bananas, plums; everything but apples.

Minutes later Luis was in the stairwell with a plum in hand, a reddish one filling in for an apple. He stood in front of his white tree, the red balls not completely erased but smeared, looking like abstract cardinals, dead ones lying on branches. He looked at the plum and drew, then erased and drew some more. He studied his new apples for so long, the shadows in the stairwell changed positions. He shook his head when he realized these new apples were as round as his old ones. He went to the stairwell window and tossed the plum out. He tried to squeeze his head between the bars when he heard Mrs. Rivera's door open and close. Then he heard something. He looked behind him and saw it roll across the floor and bang into the wall.

An apple. A Red Delicious one.

Luis ran and picked it up. He turned to Mrs. Rivera's door, stood on his toes and looked up at the peephole. He waved, yelled *thanks* then placed his ear on the door and listened. All he heard was the sound of slippers walking away.

Luis studied the apple from all sides, realizing quickly that his mother was right, the thing was not round at all.

His red chalk was the size of a rosary bead by the time Luis finished drawing his final apple. He was admiring his drawing when Vinita entered the stairwell, carrying a blue suitcase in one hand, a small purse in the other.

"Luis, your father is asleep on the sofa. In a little a while, go inside."

"Where are you going, Mami?"

"Away."

"When you coming back?"

"Soon. Do me a favor. Please, *please* stay away from your sisters when they get home."

Vinita walked up to Luis. She adjusted his shirt, combed his hair with her fingers. She moved past him and started down the stairs, her heels crashing into the marble steps, the sound blasting up and down the stairwell like gunfire. Then she stopped and returned up the steps and Luis saw that she was looking at his new apples. He lowered his eyes and fixed them on his Buster Browns, digging the left one into the floor the way he squishes cigarette butts on the street. He felt her hand on his cheek. She lifted his head, kissed him on the forehead and whispered, "They're perfect."

Then she was gone.

In the Santana Bay, Luis watched his father sleep on the sofa, in the dark except for a candle burning at the foot of the small statue of Saint Barbara sitting on a shelf. The shades were half-drawn and flapping lightly in front of the open windows. Luis moved to the center window and began to sway with a breeze that carried the scent of hot dogs from below. He listened to his father's breathing. A calmness entered the room and embraced the boy. This was how he imagined it would be like in space, floating, lost. Luis looked out the window. He saw Vinita below, standing in front of the building, chatting with a neighbor woman smoking a cigarette, the smoke surging from her then forming a grey mushroom over her coiffed hairstyle that Luis would draw later on the stairwell wall. He watched as a yellow taxi stopped in front of the building and, within seconds, swooped Vinita and her blue suitcase away. And when Luis saw his sisters walking down the block, he stepped away from the window and pulled down the painted shades of the San Juan bay. He contemplated sitting with Cruz, but the thought of the plastic on the sofa popping and waking his father stopped Luis. He began to pace. He looked at his sleeping father and suddenly felt frightened, anxious to see his mother, feeling lost without her.

Luis moved closer to the shades and stared at the murals painted on them, and slowly the boy began to feel safe, calm, guarded by the old fortress, the ocean, and the sun that would still be shining even at midnight.

# 16

Near Yankee Stadium is a park named after some poet. Joyce Kilmer. It's on the Grand Concourse running from 161$^{st}$ Street all the way to 164$^{th}$ Street where I parked the Granada.

Inside the park is a water fountain with a marble sculpture in the center named after a different poet. A German one. I forget his name. Most people do. Most people refer to the fountain as the Lorelei, a woman in a poem by this German whose name no one can remember. Vinita loves this fountain. Returns to it often. Last year we found her sitting by it with her blue suitcase, eating ice cream. She was staring at Lorelei sitting high on a rock, surrounded by mermaids, dolphins, a frog that Luis is now admiring with Vinita's picture in his hand.

"I was a kid the first time Mami brought me here." He looks up at Lorelei. "She told me once that this Lorelei jumped into the river and was changed into a goddess who could sing, and when she sang on the river, her voice hypnotized sailors and they'd fall asleep and die and wouldn't that make a great movie, Mami said—"

"Your mother was off before she left."

"She's always off before she leaves."

"This was...different...Let's check Morrisania."

"Do you have any change?"

I reach into my pocket. I hand Luis a few pennies, nickels, a dime. He moves closer to the fountain, looks at the water. He closes his eyes, whispers something, tosses the change into the fountain. A wish has been made.

We head back to the Granada then we're in it. Luis looks at the building across the street. All Hallows Institute, a high school, Catholic, all boys, the one Luis graduated from. I wanted to send him to a public school because I was cheap. But Vinita wouldn't have it.

I turn on the radio. Someone is going on about the weather, how hot it is. I ask Luis if he's hungry. He ignores me or maybe he didn't hear me. He is staring at his high school. His lips are moving, but he isn't saying anything.

I ask again if he's hungry and Luis says, "Last month I was looking for something in the back of a closet. Found an old yearbook. Junior year. There was a class picture with me and about fifteen other guys and it had our last names underneath with the initial of our first name and I started rattling off everyone's first name, remembering them all based on that initial."

"We can eat something quick or—"

"I didn't even have to stop to think. I just said their names like I had seen these guys the day before. I can't remember what I ate for breakfast today or if I ate breakfast, but I can remember names from what? Twenty-two, twenty-three years ago. And I don't know why. Those guys gave me such a hard time from day one. Because I didn't talk like them, I talked like I was from somewhere else, from anywhere but the Bronx, making fun of me thanks to you, Papi, and your damn English lessons. 'It's *coffee*, not *cawfee*.' They used to call me Mr. Pretty Talk."

This is the first I've heard of this. I don't know what to say. Something sympathetic or an apology. I open my mouth, nothing comes out.

"I'm glad you stopped being an English Professor, Papi, because you were a pain in the ass."

"I was never an English professor." I pull the Granada out into traffic. "I studied to teach Linguistics, then I met someone who did and he hated it, said you spend all day in the classroom then you go home and spend all night grading papers, planning what you're going to do in the classroom the next day, you have no free time, no life, and that was the end of that for me."

Luis points towards his high school. "Up there is where the Christian brothers lived. Live."

I start to turn right on Walton Avenue and Luis yells, "What are you doing?! It's a one-way!"

I hit the brakes.

"This is what happens when you haven't been to an area in a while," I say.

"This is what happens when you get old, Papi."

I drive down 164th Street, turn right on Gerard and drive to 168th St where the old Morrisania Hospital stands. It's a brick building, eight stories high, takes up a whole city block. Opened in the twenties, closed in the seventies when the Bronx began to go downhill. Then it sat empty for about twenty years.

I pull up the Granada in front of this hospital I went to often as a visitor. I stare at the building and wonder how it was ever a hospital. How they were able to keep such an old place sterile compared to modern hospitals that seem to clean themselves. It recently reopened as some sort of community hub. Three years ago we found Vinita standing in the front with her blue suitcase. This is where Ivonne and Luis were born. Where my mother died forty-eight years ago last week. My father couldn't continue a life here without her. He said he saw her whenever he went. He moved back to Puerto Rico and died a year later.

Luis steps out of the car. He leaves Vinita's picture behind. I pick it up, hold it out the window. I open my mouth to yell but don't. I park the car and step out with Vinita's picture. I catch up to Luis at the entrance of Morrisania. I go to put my hand on his shoulder then stop when I see his head tilted, his mouth open. I wait it out. He closes his eyes, turns to me, whispers in my ear, whispers the names of his grandparents—my parents— and something that sounds like *they're together*. And I don't say anything. Just hand him Vinita's picture and walk away. Walk until I reach the Granada. I climb inside. It feels like a hundred degrees, but I roll up the windows, turn on the radio, loud, so no one can hear me cry.

# 17

In the silence that follows the deaf girl around she can often feel her heart pounding. When her anxiety kicks in, the pounding gets louder, frightening her. Once she thought she was having a heart attack so she went to the ER at Montefiore Hospital in the Bronx. They examined her, ran some tests. Asked questions about her medical history. They didn't find anything. No irregular heartbeat. Her thyroid was fine. The hospital's ASL interpreter informed her that she had had harmless palpitations, a word she asked to be clarified. *Palpitations are heartbeats that suddenly become more conspicuous. Like someone reached into your heart and turned up the volume.* She was told her palpitations were probably caused by stress and advised her to see someone about her anxiety. And she did. She turned down an offer for a pill and opted for relaxation exercises, deep breathing, yoga, things she rarely finds time to do anymore.

Especially after reading in a magazine that anxiety is simply a reaction to stress which can be helpful, providing warnings of unpleasant things ahead and you best be prepared.

She feels palpitations now as she approaches where the hearing man waits for her, San Juan, her favorite restaurant in the Bronx that specializes in Puerto Rican cuisine; evoking the island's capital with its rustic ironwork, walls of tropical colors, wobbly tables set against a mural of El Morro, faux cobblestones beneath it.

She walks into San Juan twenty minutes late. Dinner is waiting on the table for her, not because her husband is thoughtful, but because this is their routine, hers really; texting her order to him in advance so she does not have to engage with the waiter with her deaf voice or, god forbid, slip and sign in front of the other patrons. Like anyone cares, the hearing man tells her all the time. And she realized, years ago, that no one cares, that no one is making fun of her being deaf like when she was a child, no one would dare, it's a different time. She often thinks of doing it, signing freely for the world to see, not caring what others think; she rehearses this scene often, thinks of public places to do it, like a restaurant, *this* restaurant, tonight, why not. Just wait for the right moment, she tells herself.

They eat. Everything tastes just the way her grandmother's housekeeper used to make it when she visited Puerto Rico, the way her mother Lourdes never could.

A waiter clears the table. Dessert menus appear.

She is debating between *arroz con dulce* and *budín* when it catches her eye, movement from his side of the table. She looks up from the menu. The hearing man's hands are moving, but they're not just hand movements, they're signs. He is signing. Not very well but enough for her to make out the words that tell her he finally did it, opened up the children's book for the deaf she had given him way back when, the one with color drawings of food and farm animals.

*horse likes apples*
*horse lives in barn*

He stops signing. His hands drop to the table.

She reads his lips as he says, "Now you can't tell anyone that I've never signed for you."

She looks around the restaurant. The other tables are all occupied. She is thinking this is the moment for her to sign when the waiter appears. Dessert is rejected.

The hearing man takes a swig of beer, moves his chair closer to her. He speaks quietly, slowly.

"I got your text today. About what I wanted for my birthday next week."

A swig of beer.

"I want you to be kind to me."

She is taken aback, convinced she misread his lips. Her eyes squint, her head turns slightly.

"I want you not to go postal on me for stupid shit," he says, "like when I forget to push that button on the fridge and you go for water and you get ambushed by ice cubes or because I adjust the thermostat or put away a glass on the wrong shelf. I want to go to a restaurant *I* pick out sometimes like that new Italian place I wanted to try tonight. I want for you to go to work dressed like you're going to work and not a date. I want for you to smile when I take you to visit my friends so that they stop asking me 'Who died?' That's what I want for my birthday. Take your pick."

She is horrified, certain he's talking about someone else.

"Or you can just get me a watch or some underwear, socks maybe."

She wants to get up and leave, but the weight of his words, or maybe the food, are making her nauseous, lightheaded. If she stands, she will fall over, she's sure of it.

She looks away from him. With a hand he turns her face back to him so she can see his lips.

"I've never been married before but I'm pretty sure it should be easier than this. And shouldn't we enjoy each other outside of the bedroom? At least sometimes?"

She looks down at the table. He looks away, takes a swig of beer. They sit there for a while, resigned, like two people on a subway car stuck between stations.

\\\\\

The first snowfall comes and goes as quickly as their divorce. Neither one demands anything. Through it all her father and mother are there for her; she receives checks from Javier for legal fees and daily texts from Lourdes declaring she'll come over. The texts let her know when her mother is in a good mood ("I should b there 2 hold ur hand") or not ("I need a break from ur father"). The deaf girl knows her mother will arrive and not hold her hand but take over her life, make decisions without consulting her, throw out her protein bars and feed her greasy food, complain that the bushes are out of control; all things that drive the deaf girl crazy.

Lourdes comes over and holds her hand. No meddling occurs. After an hour her mother signs that she's overwhelmed with student papers to grade then leaves with a promise to return tomorrow but never does.

While the hearing man gets his things out of the house, she stays with the deaf boy from work, on his sofa in his apartment off of the Grand Concourse with one bathroom and too many roommates. The hearing man only takes necessities with him like shoes and clothes and his Maria Callas records. They agree not to say goodbye in person so he draws a little heart on a Post-it note and leaves it on her nightstand. When she finds it, she looks at it as if it were a to-do list, an old one, long, completed, and throws it in the trash.

\\\\\

Sunday, just after sunset, the deaf girl sits slumped in a chair on her porch, wearing a coat, slippers and no makeup. Her Aunt Vinita is in front of her, sitting on her blue suitcase. Vinita watches as the wind is doing all sorts of unflattering things to the deaf girl's hair. She's thinking her niece looks as if she just crawled out of a bad car accident and collapsed on the porch, bruised and devastated. And she is. Not by the hearing man's absence but by what he left her with—insecurities she had always been able to keep at bay. But now, she signs to Vinita, they are in her face all day long as if he had highlighted them with bright-colored markers, loud and vulgar as neon signs. She always saw herself as a catch, a prize, a joy to be with. Now all that is shattered, her confidence gone. Not even the kind words from Vinita help. The women hug. The deaf girl watches her aunt pick up her suitcase and stand at the edge of the porch for some time. Then she is gone.

The next day, the deaf girl's rage arrives and obliterates her devastation. She is so furious at the hearing man she can't feel anything else for weeks, riding trains sitting down, her head buried in *The New York Times* pretending to read, afraid to make eye contact with anyone. When the grief finally arrives, she is at work returning from lunch. She walks along the wall of diamond ads trying not to look at The Blonde Woman when she notices it, a new ad, in Spanish, for *Vogue España*. The woman in this ad looks like the deaf girl: her hair black, her skin dark, smooth; she is admiring a diamond ring on her finger; a dark man stands behind her smiling with perfect teeth, his chin on her shoulder, arms around her small waist. The deaf girl stares at the ad too long and she feels herself falling into a black hole. A chill goes through her and suddenly it feels as though the temperature has dropped in the room. She shivers. She folds her arms across herself, tightly, but the shivering continues. Moments later she's hunched over a table of diamonds, loupe in her eye, the damn thing filling with tears, the lens blurring and she's drowning in a sea of diamonds, unsure if she's awake or not.

She takes time off from work. She dyes her hair blonde.

And, for the first time since he left, she cleans her house.

Then she redecorates.

In their bedroom she removes all traces of color: red lamp shades become black, floral curtains a plain ivory. She paints over the teal blue walls she once told him she could never live without, paints every wall a different shade of grey, the moldings white, the beam black; a color scheme deliberately lifted out of *Guernica*, reframed and hanging back in the foyer.

At night she leaves the blinds half open so moonlight can fill the room. She turns off the lights and lies in her new bed surrounded by new pillows, sheets, blankets. She can't smell his Cool Water cologne anymore thanks to the paint fumes still in the air. She looks around the room, completely dissatisfied with the colorless world before her but pleased that she has defeated the moonlight, that everything looks just the way it does in the daylight. She stares up at the black beam until she drifts into sleep, into dreams about *Guernica* and burning barns with gored ivory horses and angry black bulls with tails of flames the color of charcoal; the grieving woman with the dead baby has been replaced by her grandmother Dolores playing jacks with jacks made of diamonds, always halting the game to introduce the young boys she's playing with, her sons, she says, all naked, all covered in grey placenta, their umbilical cords still attached. It isn't until the deaf girl has the beam removed one Saturday that the *Guernica* dreams begin to subside.

And when she gets tired of pacing her empty house and the silence and stillness that greets her in every room, she asks the deaf boy at work to move into her guest room. He agrees. The day of his arrival, she goes around the house opening windows. Winter is gone. Her neighbors are sitting on their porches again enjoying the sun. She's about to smile when she remembers something. She goes to her computer and begins to type. An hour later she is looking at a list of her house rules that is a page long, things like *Coffee cup handles must point right* and *Towels must be grouped by color (see towel folding instructions below)*; a section on *Non-Negotiable Thermostat Settings* broken down by season, etc., etc. She rereads the list to make sure she hasn't forgotten anything. Halfway through it—not even half—she becomes appalled. And when she reads *Make sure towel hemmed edges are hidden underneath fluffy folded edges*, she is nauseated. She rewrites the list until it's short enough to fit on a Post-it note then sticks it on his bedroom door: *Do whatever the fuck you want.*

Her doorbell rings and the foyer light over *Guernica* flashes three times like a distress signal for help. She runs and opens the door and there is the deaf boy, more than twenty pounds lighter, smiling, a box of protein bars in his hands, suitcases at his feet. Behind him a yellow cab, the trunk open, the driver pulling out small moving boxes. And even though she had seen him the day before, at work, she hugs him now as if she had not seen anyone in years.

# 18

Before we moved to the farm, I was a thin woman with brown eyes. *Beautiful eyes*, Ben called them when we first met in his office three years ago. I had selected him out of an insurance catalog after my regular dentist retired. I choose Ben simply because his office was the shortest commute from my home.

In the past my dentists have always been older men with grey hair or no hair, often with a beer belly, that remind you of a captain of a ship or a priest or someone's grandfather. So I didn't expect Ben to be so good looking. He *was* older but with the body of a much younger man who took care of himself, clearly was at the gym often. His hair was brown and curly, the sideburns tinged with grey.

Sitting in a dental chair is awkward, not the best position to be in when you meet someone for the first time. Ben entered the room saying hello. I said hello before he was standing before me. When he finally did, we both froze for a few seconds. Ben opened his mouth but didn't say anything. He tilted his head slightly like he was trying to figure out if he had met me before. I looked at him the same way. This is the moment in my soap operas where music begins to play, the screen fades to black, a commercial plays, and you sit on the sofa wondering how it is going to play out. He then told me I had beautiful eyes. I thanked him. I noticed he wasn't wearing a wedding ring when a dental assistant entered the room to drop something off or pick something up then left. Ben proceeded to go over my X-rays that someone had taken earlier. I was pleased to hear I had a few cavities. That I would have to return for multiple visits for Ben to take care of.

On each visit my outfits became tighter, the cleavage a little more exposed. There was harmless flirtation on both our parts. Then, on one visit, I was sitting in the waiting room while a staff member was training a new receptionist. A call came in for Ben. A message was taken. Then I overheard *That's Julia, his fiancée*. I let out a long sigh. I took the long, bulky sweater on my lap and slipped it on to cover all my business. For my remaining visits, I remained pleasant but curbed the flirtation even if Ben didn't.

On my final visit Ben mentioned a restaurant in Manhattan he was going to be at that night to have dinner with friends. He didn't outright invite me. He just said the name of the restaurant and location half a dozen times as well as the time he would be there. I got up from the dental chair, gathered my things and casually said, "Will your fiancée be there?" Before he could answer, I left. Later that night I arrived at the restaurant and there were no friends there. Just Ben, waiting, hoping I'd show up, he told me later. I told him I wasn't going to sleep with him. He laughed, I laughed. We had drinks, dinner. I went home. These friendly dinners continued for a while until we spiraled into bad behavior and, once again, I was caught up in the same drama, same storyline, different leading man.

And now here I am on a farm, no longer thin, with a toothache that comes and goes, but I don't tell Ben about it because I don't want to sit in a dental chair I don't fit in anymore.

This morning at breakfast, Ben says my eyes look sad, lifeless. He says this as I'm about to say grace. I pretend I don't hear him. As I thank God for this and that, Ben coughs, adjusts his tie, shifts in his seat in one of his gloomy polyester suits, the dark grey one, the one that looks like he tossed and turned in ashes all night. I finish grace. We do the sign of the cross. Ben picks up a piece of bacon and chews with that same stoic look the horses always wear. Then, like every morning, we begin our morning routine, this ritual of silent accusations that begins with a sigh, a look, a gesture over the table, the same wood table where we made love when we first arrived on the farm.

Ben finishes breakfast. He leaves the kitchen. I hear him walk through our ranch home. I hear water running. He's brushing his teeth. He gargles. He stops at his computer to stare at photos of naked women that look a lot like I used to look. Thin. He stares until he relieves himself loud enough for me to hear. He goes out the door. His pickup truck comes alive, drives off. I look over the breakfast table. Dirty dishes and silverware. Half-empty cups of coffee.

The place setting for silence undisturbed, unnoticed once again. I sit there drinking coffee until our cleaning woman appears in the doorway. An older woman who only speaks to me when she arrives ("Good morning") and when she leaves ("Good night"). I leave her in the kitchen and go out to the porch. Workers wave at me. I wave back. I stand there in the heat drinking coffee, thinking of plans to escape this life, ways to execute those plans.

When a worker is done feeding the horses, I walk to the stable. Inside, I move from stall to stall greeting the horses by name. I didn't know how to ride a horse until my son taught me during our first week here. He learned to ride young at the summer camps for the rich his father insisted on sending him to despite my disapproval, my fears that he would become spoiled. Raul was a pro horse rider by the time he was ten years old, always declaring he wanted to be a jockey or cowboy. He couldn't wait to move to this farm. After a month here, Raul grew bored with the place. Now he flies off every chance he gets. He's twenty-five and has never had a real job.

Though we're not legally obligated, his father and I continue to give Raul money, out of guilt or stupidity. If Raul were a character on one my soap operas, he'd be the entitled rich kid who believes the world revolves around him, always busy doing a lot of nothing, the annoying character you yell at from your sofa every time he appears on screen.

My favorite horse is a black Arabian colt named Bailey who made my training a breeze. He is calm, patient. Easy to ride. Raul had told me a horse's center of gravity is always shifting with every step it takes, every change of gait, and it's up to the rider, not the horse, to adapt as the animal goes from a walk to a trot to a canter to a gallop. I adapted very well. Bailey and I moved as one. But since I've gained weight, Bailey won't go past a walk.

Bailey walks us out of the stable. We walk past the silo. We go around the main house and Bailey is startled by white sheets on the clotheslines blowing in the wind like ghosts. I whisper something to him. He settles down. We move on.

The farm feels like a small town with the buildings and streets erased, the noise hushed for good like a radio with its cord cut off. I lead Bailey down a trail or maybe he's leading me. I begin to hum just so I can hear something other than wind.

Not too far from the main house is a spot steps away from our small lake where I had asked Ben when we arrived to plant daisies. That spring I went to greet the daisies and found white roses instead. I think about the daisies I wanted as Bailey walks me along the roses. We go by the blueberry field in full bloom. Two male workers pass by carrying their lunches. I greet them with a nod because I don't know their names. I used to learn the workers' names.

However, unlike the horses who never go away, the workers come and go quickly, most of them drifters Ben meets in town. Some only last a week or two or however long it takes to realize what a shit town this is. Now I don't learn anyone's name.

At the edge of the lake, Bailey dips his head for a drink of water. On the other side of the lake is a male worker sitting on the grass. He is about half a city block away. He is eating a sandwich, staring into the lake. His auburn hair is longer than mine. He looks early thirties. Tall, tan, muscular. He puts the sandwich down, removes his red tank top. Every muscle is defined, covered in sweat. He picks up the sandwich and continues eating, completely oblivious of Bailey and me.

Bailey lifts his head and neighs. He is done drinking, ready to go, surely anxious to get me off his back. I hear a voice yell. *Hello.* The shirtless worker is waving. Workers never talk to me so I assume he's waving at someone else. I look behind me, around me. There is no one there. By the time I decide to wave back, the worker is putting on his tank top, walking around the lake, then he is standing in front of us. I introduce myself.

I'm Jesus, he says.

How was your lunch?

I'm not sure. Someone with an extra sandwich was kind enough to share. I just couldn't figure out if it was chicken or turkey. Who's this?

Bailey.

Jesus puts his hand on top of Bailey's head, runs it down to his muzzle. He looks up at me and says something out of the Bible, some quote. I squint, confused.

If you bring forth what is within you, it will save you, he says.

His words are familiar. I try to place them.

Then he says, If you do not bring forth what is within you, it will destroy you.

I remember the words now, from Catholic school, from *The Gospel of Thomas* and I ask again what is his name and this time he doesn't just say *Jesus*, he says *Jesus Christ* and I realize then he is no worker but a resident from Coghill, a religious retreat house in the next town. Run by priests helping people who are "off," who stay there until they are well or they can't afford to pay anymore. The previous farm owner informed Ben and I that Coghill residents tend to wander off and find themselves on the farm, confusing it for a park but *don't worry, they're harmless.* Since we've been here, we've had plenty of Coghill residents stop by. Many have even stayed for a meal. Some think they're someone they're not, others are simply indifferent towards the world. Or plain sad.

Jesus turns towards the lake and looks out. His arms glisten in the afternoon light. He talks about the state of the world and prayer and sin and stuff like that. I interject when I can. Every so often he drops a quote from the Bible. Once I'm convinced he's harmless, I get off Bailey who seems to sigh audibly with relief. I stand next to Jesus. We look across the lake, chatting away. It is the most adult conversation

I've had since I left the Bronx two years ago. When he sees my wedding ring, he breaks into a fragmented speech made up of quotes from the Testaments, Old and New. When he's done, he falls silent. His eyes move across my face then up, down, and across again. There's nothing romantic about it. It's like he's looking into a computer screen, searching for something. Suddenly his eyes open wide like he found it, maybe a Wikipedia entry, about me, that he proceeds to read out loud and it's so damn accurate, and sad in so many ways, that I want to cry.

# 19

**M**ovies. That was always Vinita's thing. An obsession that began in 1948 on her eighteenth birthday when an uncle took her to the Candlelight Theatre in San Juan, Puerto Rico to see her first movie, *La calle sin sol*, starring Antonio Vilar and Amparo Rivelles as a man and woman who fall in love; all's well until his dark past catches up with him and he becomes a suspect in a murder. For ninety-five minutes, Vinita was captivated by the story that unfolded in black and white on the largest screen she had ever seen. At one point the audience broke into applause, they cheered. Vinita looked around the theatre, at the patrons' faces, their eyes never wavering from the screen and suddenly she didn't want to be in her seat, she wanted to be on the screen to feed her desire to be looked at. As a child, while her sister Lourdes buried herself in schoolbooks, Vinita spent her time doing what she could to be the center of attention wherever she went: family gatherings, church events, schoolyards. And as she grew older so did her need to be looked at and applauded, appearing in local festivals, beauty pageants, mostly because she enjoyed it but also to distract herself from the sadness that consumed her at night when she lay in bed and looked across at an empty bed. A bed that once belonged to her sister who had moved to the States to attend Columbia University.

And for a year, every time a new movie opened at the Candlelight Theatre, Vinita was there, always. One night she called her sister in the Bronx and told her she wanted to be in the movies. Lourdes was supportive, encouraging Vinita to come to New York City and stay with her, enroll in an acting class. "It'd be great to share a room again, Vinita." With her mother's encouragement and financial support, Vinita Velez left Puerto Rico at the end of August 1950.

She was twenty when she stepped off a plane at LaGuardia Airport, greeted by Lourdes and her new boyfriend, Javier. On the drive to the Bronx, Vinita took in the view of the streets of Queens, the Manhattan skyline in the distance, so much concrete everywhere, so little green compared to the island. They stopped at a red light. To her left, in a restaurant window, Vinita saw a sign. *No Dogs or Puerto Ricans Allowed*. Vinita looked towards the front seat. Javier was changing radio stations. Lourdes was looking ahead rambling about what they'd do tomorrow. Vinita looked over at the sign again. White men and women were going in and out of the restaurant. Lourdes had mentioned that there were places in New York City that weren't very warm towards Puerto Ricans, places she knew to avoid. When Vinita asked *how do you know what places to avoid*, Lourdes said *you'll know* and Vinita wasn't sure what her sister meant until she saw this sign now. The traffic light changed to green. The car moved. The sign was gone and then Javier was dropping them off in front of Lourdes' apartment building in the Bronx. For the first time since stepping off the plane, Vinita began to relax when she saw Puerto Ricans all around her, on the street, going in and out of the apartment building, many exchanging greetings with Lourdes who would say to them, proudly, *this is my sister Vinita, just flew in from Puerto Rico*; all of them hugging Vinita as if they'd known her for years. Javier said he had things to take care of but would be back that night. Before he drove off, Lourdes and he engaged in a brief conversation. Vinita was stunned when her sister began speaking to Javier in fluent English without a trace of a Spanish accent. In Puerto Rico, English was taught as a second language in school, however, most people, like Vinita, weren't fluent because they didn't continue speaking English outside the classroom, except for those who were planning to continue their studies in the States like her sister. Lourdes' English was always much better than Vinita's, but it wasn't fluent and her accent was as thick as Vinita's. But not anymore.

Javier placed Vinita's two brown suitcases on the curb, said goodbye and drove off. The sisters climbed the apartment stairwell with suitcases in hand. Each time they passed an apartment, Lourdes mentioned who lived in it. The building was mostly Puerto Ricans, but there were some Italians, some Irish, all friendly.

Lourdes had a small, one-bedroom apartment that seem to have more books than furniture. She had graduated with honors from Columbia and was now a graduate student at NYU.

"And some of my classes are in that building," Lourdes said as she pointed to a red brick building. They were walking through Greenwich Village eating hot dogs. Lourdes mentioned she had asked around about acting classes for Vinita. There was one within walking distance from campus that would be perfect because they could ride in together on the train. Sometime later, after reviewing a schedule of classes, Vinita enrolled in an acting class and then they were sitting on a bench eating ice cream in Washington Square Park. It was just after 2:00 p.m. when Lourdes said, "What do you want to do now?"

"See a movie."

Vinita had only seen Spanish films in Puerto Rico. She was completely clueless about American cinema so she let Lourdes pick out the film. Her sister informed Vinita that since she wanted to be in the movies then she should see a film about the movies. An hour later they were sitting in a movie theatre watching *Sunset Boulevard*. The first thing Vinita noticed was that a lot more money was spent on this movie than the Spanish ones she had seen; the visuals more stunning, sets more elaborate, costumes more detailed. All of it playing out on the largest screen she had ever seen, the sound clear and lush. By the time Norma Desmond arrived at Paramount Studios, you would've thought Vinita was watching a thriller the way her heart was racing. And when Norma walked arm in arm with Cecil B. DeMille through a sound stage with cameras and lights, Lourdes leaned into her sister's ear and whispered, "Breathe." Vinita had stepped off the plane about six hours earlier in this new city, yet before the movie even ended, she was already planning to move to Hollywood.

They were walking towards the subway going on and on in Spanish about *Sunset Boulevard* when they ran into a woman who was in one of Lourdes' classes. Her sister introduced Vinita who shook the woman's hand then stepped back as Lourdes and the woman carried on in English. Again, Vinita was amazed at her sister's perfect English, not once stumbling over a word the way she used to do in Puerto Rico. Her classmate said goodbye and walked away. Vinita asked Lourdes how did her English get so good. *Cruz Santana*, Lourdes said, *the Puerto Rican in apartment 6B, two floors above me, the only one in the building with a television, been here since he was a child*; a seamstress in a dress factory in Manhattan, makes dresses. "Maybe he can get you a job. Anyway, he studied English or something, and in his spare time he helps Puerto Ricans clean up their English so they can blend in more, he says, avoid discrimination, get better jobs. And when we met in our stairwell and I heard him speak English so beautifully, I told him if I could speak English like him, I'd raise my hand more in my classes and that's when he offered to help me and, well, here I am—"

"I want to meet him."

That night, at Vinita's welcome party in her sister's apartment, there were so many people one could barely move. "And this is Vinita," Lourdes said to Cruz when he arrived. The trim, handsome man, twenty, stood there speechless, staring at Vinita who looked like a beauty-pageant contestant in her blue satin dress with a square neckline, tight bodice, cinched waist and full skirt that stopped just past her knees as it should have, Cruz thought, for it would've been a crime for the satin to descend any further and conceal Vinita's gorgeous legs. They talked about Puerto Rico, briefly, in Spanish until Vinita began responding in English with her thick accent.

She struggled to remember the English equivalent of certain words when she finally laughed and confessed to Cruz that she would like him to help her the way he had helped Lourdes. After that night, after her acting class ended and Cruz got home from work, they would work together to improve her English, eliminate her accent, expand her vocabulary. Do away with slang. It was always *want to* or *going to*, never *wanna* or *gonna*; all lessons he would pass on, years later, to their children.

Vinita's English improved quickly through vocal exercises and watching television shows like *The Lone Ranger* and *Dragnet* in Cruz's apartment. "Just watch their lips and jaw," Cruz would say. "Copy the movement, repeat the words." Some weeks the English lessons continued at a movie theatre with Cruz sitting next to Vinita as she repeated, in whispers, whatever an actress said on screen. When something didn't sound right, Cruz would correct Vinita, whispering things into her ear like "Drop your jaw a little more." Vinita enjoyed the lessons in the theatre, but what she enjoyed even more was discovering an actress she was unfamiliar with, feeling her emotions, repeating her words. One week it was Bette Davis in *All About Eve*, the next week Hedy Lamarr in *Samson and Delilah*, the first color film Vinita had seen; it so dazzled her that she went back to see it, alone, again and again.

During this time, in his apartment, after the English lessons ended, Cruz would teach Vinita how to sew on his Singer machine. Eventually he helped get her a job at his dress factory, not so much because he wanted to help. He simply wanted to be around her all the time. But she quickly got bored being hunched over a sewing machine all day where no one could see her. She quit and found a job as a waitress at a malt shop near her acting class where she was on display all day long in a tight pink-and-white uniform, arriving home late at night with pockets full of tips and telephone numbers from men.

Three months later Vinita's English was fluent, the accent gone. The lessons stopped. But Cruz loved that Vinita still returned to his apartment almost every night. Not to see him but his television. He always had food and beverages ready, but she ate like a bird then sipped on water. *I have to watch my figure*, Vinita always said, *I read the film camera adds weight.*

They'd sit there on opposite ends of his sofa in silence or laughing at the screen every night except Mondays when she wouldn't come over because *I Love Lucy* was on. Vinita was convinced that if she listened to Ricky Ricardo's accent, even for a second, hers would return.

Then they began sleeping together. Maybe it was because Vinita felt obligated, felt like she owed him for all the English lessons. Or maybe she finally saw Cruz as something other than her English tutor. After all he was an attractive man, turning heads every time he visited her at the malt shop. Not to mention their evenings were often interrupted by a knock on his door, pretty neighborhood women wanting to visit, women he politely turned away.

After they made love Vinita would always spend the night with Cruz. And she'd talk on and on. About anything. A film, an actor, her mother, the subway, or, lately, a girlfriend from her acting class who moved to California last month to continue her studies, to get into the movies, how happy her friend sounded on the phone when they spoke recently.

One night, after the lovemaking was over, Vinita was silent for a long time. Cruz assumed she had fallen asleep and closed his eyes. Then Vinita got out of bed and began to get dressed in the dark. Cruz turned on the lamp on the nightstand. He looked at her, confused. She said she had things she had to take care of. She finished dressing then sat at the edge of the bed next to him.

"This has been fun," Vinita said.

"Are you done with me?"

"Hmm?"

"You said *has been*."

"Did I?"

He nodded.

She giggled.

"Damn grammar," she said. "I'm regressing. I meant *is*."

Vinita leaned in, kissed him. Then she was gone so fast that he wondered if he had dreamt the whole thing.

The next evening Cruz had dinner and the television ready for them. When Vinita never showed up, he began to wonder if *I Love Lucy* was on, if it was Monday already. He went over to the wall calendar. It was Thursday. A few minutes later he was knocking at apartment 4C. Lourdes opened the door, a book in hand, a pencil behind her ear. Cruz looked past her into the apartment.

"She's gone," Lourdes said.

"Where?"

"California."

Cruz leaned in and turned his head to the side. Lourdes repeated herself because she thought Cruz hadn't heard her. But he had. She was saying something else that he didn't hear because he was already climbing the stairs back to his apartment.

\\\\\

For days Cruz carried on like a child whose favorite amusement park, the one he's been going to every night except Mondays, had closed for good. He wandered the city after work like a lost tourist in a daze, never sure where he was or where he was going. Sometimes he'd find himself sitting in a movie theatre but not sure how he got there. Sometimes he'd find himself across the street from Vinita's acting class, waiting, as if she were inside instead of on the other side of the country. Sometimes he'd sit on one end of the sofa with the television going loudly but not hearing a word.

A week later Cruz returned to see Lourdes. She made them coffee. While Javier slept in the other room, Cruz sipped on his coffee as Lourdes gave him more details. Vinita was living in Hollywood, sleeping on the sofa of her friend from acting class. At night Vinita worked at a diner. During the day she did extra work at Warner Brothers. Her friend's agent, Jeanine Jones a.k.a. J.J., now represented Vinita as well. J.J. kept Vinita busy with interviews, auditions, lots of hand modeling and extra work. That was all Lourdes knew. After that, Cruz would check in with Lourdes for any updates on Vinita, but it was always the same: Vinita was making the rounds. Meanwhile Cruz was unable to sleep, to watch television, to take interest in any of the women who continued to knock on his door. Then one day Cruz was arriving home from work as Lourdes was on her way to a class.

"I just called you," Lourdes said.

"What's wrong?"

"Vinita. She got a screen test with Twentieth Century Fox."

"What's that? Like an interview?"

"Sort of. Except it's in front of a camera. They have you do a scene. All you have to do is look good on film, Vinita said, and everything else they can take care of with classes and stuff—my god! My little sister might do this after all."

Two weeks later Vinita informed Lourdes she was offered a studio contract. She was twenty-one. Vinita said that due to her pale skin and fluent English they were going to bury the Puerto Rican in her, drop the Velez. Her new name was going to be Vinita Vale or Vaughn or something like that, they were still deciding. She was to arrive tomorrow at Fox at 8:00 a.m. to sign her contract, tour the studio, have lunch, confirm measurements in Wardrobe, meet department heads, etc., etc. The excitement in Vinita's voice was palpable. She was frightened too. "Everything is happening so fast," Vinita said. Lourdes congratulated her sister over and over, then Vinita said she had to go, she had to call their mother and give her the news.

Lourdes did not hear from Vinita again. She kept leaving messages with her roommate who always said she was out.

"Maybe she's making a movie," Cruz said.

"Maybe."

Two weeks later—after still no word from Vinita—Cruz was standing in an apartment building in Hollywood knocking on Vinita's door with a suitcase in hand, a winter coat in the other. The door swung open and Vinita stood there. She was unrecognizable to him. Every time he had seen her, she was dressed as if she were going to a fancy dinner or cocktail party even if she was just going to be sitting at his kitchen table learning English or in front of the television. And now here she was with no makeup, her hair all over the place, wearing slippers and an oversized bathrobe. There wasn't a hint of surprise in her face, as if she had just seen him yesterday and they were still in his Bronx apartment. Cruz hadn't told Lourdes he was coming yet Vinita appeared as if she was expecting him. She turned around and walked into the apartment leaving the door open. Cruz hesitated for a moment, walked inside and closed the door. He sat his suitcase in the entry way, threw his coat on it then walked into the living room. Vinita was looking out a window with a partial view of the Hollywood Hills. Even though it was late afternoon, the sofa was still made up as a bed with a pillow and sheets. All the windows were open. A metal fan was running on a desk in the corner. Cruz moved slowly around the room peeking down a hallway and the kitchen, trying to determine if they were alone. Once he was convinced they were, he said something about the weather, how warm and sunny it was there, how cold it was back in the Bronx.

"It all fell through," Vinita whispered.

On the day of the contract signing, her first stop was the wardrobe department to confirm her measurements were the same as they were in her screen test a month earlier. They weren't. Vinita was surprised since she still had been eating like a bird. The wardrobe woman said to Vinita that she didn't look well and asked if she was okay.

"I threw up this morning and still feel a little nausea," Vinita said to the woman. "I'm just nervous to be here."

"You're not nervous," the woman said, "you're pregnant."

And with that the woman left to make a phone call. When she returned, she told Vinita the rest of her day was canceled, explaining that due to her condition, the studio was unable to sign her at this time. "But once you have the baby, give us a call. They'll be happy to sign then, I mean, they're still talking about your screen test." The woman instructed Vinita to make sure she gets back into shape and returns in the form of her original measurements which she wrote down on a piece of paper and handed to Vinita who was standing there in tears.

"Oh honey," the woman said, "there's no need to cry. Nine months will go by in no time."

Vinita turned from the window and looked at Cruz. He moved closer to her. She opened her bathroom and stood there naked, revealing her small but noticeable bump. She wanted to tell him she had considered getting rid of it, but the guilt embedded in her from her Catholic upbringing had prevented her. She wanted to tell him that at first she wasn't sure it was his but perhaps someone she had met at the malt shop back in New York. It wasn't until the doctor confirmed her due date and she did the math that she knew it was his.

But when Cruz placed his hand on her stomach, Vinita said nothing. She closed her eyes as he leaned in to kiss her. Her right hand remained in her bathrobe pocket clutching a piece of paper with her measurements on it. A paper she would look at tomorrow and wonder how the holes got there, the ones her nails were now making.

# 20

A woman sits alone in a favorite diner.

There's a blue suitcase at her feet.

On the table, a half-eaten spinach salad, a glass of water.

Nearby a newspaper open to the movie section.

A waitress appears with cherry pie.

The woman takes one bite then sprinkles salt over the pie, lots of it.

The pie is covered with a white napkin.

Like a corpse on a gurney.

She digs through her purse, pushing things aside.

A lipstick is found, applied, returned to its place.

The newspaper is picked up, the date noticed.

It's her son's birthday today.

*Must call him, must find a phone.*

She gestures for the check, looks out the window.

Her eyes dart up and down and across the street.

Nothing is familiar.

A cup of coffee is ordered.

And she sits there for a long time.

Trying to remember where she is and where she is going.

# 21

"There's no parking, just stop here."

I double park the Granada in front of a brick house. Luis gets out. He goes up the porch steps and rings the doorbell. The deaf girl opens the door. I don't recognize her. Months ago she had blonde hair, then she had cut it short by the time I ran into her a week later. She is no longer blonde. The hair is longer.

The deaf girl waves to me from the doorway. I wave back. Luis goes inside. I look up the block. Further down and across the street is Luis' apartment building. I decide to tell him to go home. Go do whatever he's going to do for his birthday. I'll keep searching for Vinita on my own. Twenty minutes later Luis gets in the car next to me. He's chewing on something that looks like a large, flat Tootsie Roll. "It's a chocolate protein bar," he says. Asks if I want a bite. No thanks.

"The deaf girl said Mami hasn't been here in months."

"How is she?"

"She seems fine. She's got some guy living there. A roommate."

"Good, she's not alone."

"And she gave me fifty bucks for my birthday then apologized for not putting it in a card, like I care."

"What else did she say?"

"She doesn't say anything, she signs. I asked her if she remembered that time when we were kids and you adults forgot us in the Bronx Zoo and we couldn't communicate and her response was how can I forget that was every day of my marriage—"

A back passenger door opens. The deaf girl slides in. Luis and I turn back and look at her. She begins to sign. Something about her mother and Vinita. She signs some more.

*cemetery*

Sometime later I'm turning off of Jerome Avenue into Woodlawn Cemetery. Drive past the iron gates. The place is like a huge park. Roads going everywhere. Luis tells me to turn left. The deaf girl points in the opposite direction so I turn right.

"I think it's up ahead," Luis says.

I park on the side of the road. There is no one around. We get out and follow the deaf girl. We walk the grounds for some time, sweating. My feet begin to hurt so I stop walking and they look at me. I point to my feet, make a face. The deaf girl gives me an understanding nod, Luis rolls his eyes. I lean to rest against a mausoleum. The grey stone like a block of fire against my ass. I pull away from it. It's huge, this mausoleum, like a little stone house for four. Luis starts going on about how "Woodlawn has one of the most distinguished collections of historic mausoleums in the country" like he is some tour guide or a salesman trying to sell me a mausoleum. His hands are signing badly I'm sure, because the deaf girl shakes her head at him and looks away.

"How do you know so much about mausoleums?" I say.

"I used to work here, remember?"

"I don't."

"It was just for a few months."

"What did you do?"

The deaf girl claps her hands loudly and starts walking. We follow her.

"I used to do tours here," Luis says, "and when there were no tours, they'd have me clean up leaves and garbage from the graves. You'd be surprised by the shit people drop here like they were at Coney Island. Anyway I couldn't keep working here. There were too many dead people talking to me at the same time, too many signs to interpret, it was exhausting—ah hah, here it is."

Luis taps the deaf girl's shoulder. She stops walking and turns to face him. Luis moves and stands in front of a headstone that says *Herman Melville*.

"Mami loves Herman," Luis says. "She used to read *Moby-Dick* to me." I don't remember Vinita reading *Moby-Dick*.

The deaf girl and I watch Luis look behind Herman's headstone like he's expecting Vinita to be sitting back there reading *Moby-Dick*. He looks disappointed for a second then begins to sign and speak. "When I used to work here, I'd take breaks and hang out with Herman and I swear sometimes I could hear ocean waves and seagulls and once I could hear a thunderstorm even though the sun was out, the sky was blue... 'But faith, like a jackal, feeds among the tombs, and even from these dead doubts she gathers her most vital hope...'" Luis stops signing and whispers something that sounds like *Call me Ishmael*.

A breeze ruffles the leaves above us and we look up.

# 22

"Dr. Lourdes Ramos is the best art history professor I've ever had." Though she had never heard anyone say this, Lourdes convinced herself that they sat around, her students, and said such things, in cafeterias or bookstores, skimming through art books, sipping coffee. This thought tumbled through her head as she drifted through the halls of the art building at Hunter College, doing her best not to make eye contact with the students. What made her a successful professor, she believed, was her unwavering aloofness, a trait she made sure was always on display. Lourdes knew her students feared her, many even hated her, she was sure of that. She watched them now, these young men and women passing her by in the hall, some with pierced ears, others with eccentric looks, their locks dipped in colors lifted out of crayon boxes, the odd colors, the ones that even she, as a child, didn't know what to do with. While some of her colleagues met with students after classes, at bars and coffee houses to engage, she was certain, in heated debates about Impressionism or their favorite Monet painting, Lourdes avoided participating in such off-campus activities.

"You should make an effort," Javier said to her once, "to connect with them."

"I have office hours," Lourdes said. "Students can come by every Tuesday between 2:00 and 3:00 and discuss whatever they want."

"Do they?"

"Of course," she lied.

A colleague passed Lourdes in the hall. They exchanged nods and Lourdes continued drifting, examining, making sense of these young students rushing by in peculiar clothing that said to her, *Look at me, I'm special.* She understood them. She too, at their age, made herself up as she went along, out of regrets and resentments mixed with whatever the latest fashion was.

Lourdes stepped into her office. She went through her mail then tossed it in the trash.

She checked her voicemail. No messages. She couldn't remember the last time she had a message and she wondered now, like always, why she even bothered checking her voicemail anymore. Everything was done via email now and that distressed her, never hearing a voice on a message, even a short one like *Call me, we need to talk.* But no one needed to talk anymore and this made her sad now. She tried to push the feeling away, but it kept jabbing at her from all sides until she surrendered. Lourdes closed her office door and sat there, crying, scanning her emails, writing the same response to each one: *Call me.*

Lourdes wiped her eyes and opened her office door. She began to color her cheeks with peach blush, lots of it; the only color able to off-set the cruel green tones cast by the fluorescent lights that followed her around all day. Her colleagues were walking by her door, paired off in twos and threes, discussing evening plans. Lourdes was never included anymore after years of turning down invitations. When she was asked once at a department gathering what her biggest regret was, she lied and said, "Not having more children." It seemed like the best answer to give, the one she felt would gain her the most sympathy. Her biggest regret, however, was her inability to make friends, to show interest in people outside her family, to carry on a conversation; things that contributed to her realization that she spent too much time with Javier, too much time at home, her head buried in books or student papers, the occasional magazine. Javier often said they should socialize more. "We should," she'd say. But they never did.

"Don't you have a class now?" a female colleague asked, her head suspended in the doorway. Lourdes nodded, pleased that someone had spoken to her. She opened her mouth to engage her colleague, but the woman had already vanished.

Standing at the front of her classroom now, Lourdes kept her pacing to a minimum during her lecture, making sure she never wandered too far from the podium. Her notes—on blue index cards—were stacked neatly in front of her. Though Lourdes had not read from an index card or even glanced at one in over ten years, she felt comforted by the cards, convinced she'd be lost without them.

"Charles Baudelaire, a French art critic, once wrote," Lourdes said from the podium, 'Romanticism is precisely situated neither in choice of subject nor exact truth, but in the way of feeling...'"

Her monotone voice continued and she heard it but didn't recognize it, feeling as if it were coming from a less interesting professor standing behind her. Her eyes wandered the classroom making sure never to rest too long on any particular student, especially the ones hiding behind laptops. Lately it was a challenge for Lourdes to ignore the persistent tapping of fingers slamming against keypads. It wasn't the tapping that distracted her but the idea that her students were not taking notes but updating their Facebook page or searching Craigslist for a free futon or typing over and over *I'm so fucking bored.* Who could blame them, she thought. Even she was bored with her own lecture, with the whole idea of Romanticism, a movement that emphasized in its time, for the first time, strong emotions as part of the aesthetic experience and what a ridiculous idea that was, she had written, years ago, on one of her index cards. Suddenly, Lourdes began to rush through her lecture, anxious for it to end. Her slide show of art from the Romantic period—Fuseli and Delacroix mostly—was now at the mercy of her twitching finger, flashing rapidly on the screen, making her feel as if she were on drugs, as if she were drowning in the very artwork she was talking about. Lourdes ended the slide show abruptly and turned on the lights. There was a silence in the classroom as everyone waited for their eyes to adjust to the light. The students studied Lourdes. She knew they were trying to determine if her lecture was indeed over. They were waiting for her usual cue and, after a few seconds, she gave it to them: Lourdes raised her left eyebrow, a gesture that affected the room like a magic wand. Her students came back to life with a feistiness that only surfaced during the Q&A portion of the class. They were disputing her lecture now with questions that challenged her claims about Romanticism. Lourdes defended herself with arguments she had memorized in grad school, quoting facts and figures, citing sources, her voice soft, toneless, as if she were reading a camera manual. At the end of the class, there was still no consensus in the room, but Lourdes didn't care. She left the classroom with a small smile hidden under her scarf, content that her students had done exactly what she had wanted, engaged in the obliteration of Romanticism.

Lourdes spent the next hour running on subway platforms, jumping from one train to another until she stepped off the 1 train on Houston Street. She made her way up to the street and began to walk briskly in the cold towards the Film Forum, clinging to her bag.

She arrived at the theatre with her mind drained, her body exhausted, ready more for a nap than a movie. She found someone there that resembled Javier, a younger Javier, staring at a movie poster, rocking back and forth. He looked almost like he had when she'd first met him, his hair dark without a trace of grey, still messy but in a cool way. His black coat was open, revealing a cranberry sweater she had never seen. It hung loosely, disguising his large belly.

"You like?" Javier said.

"What did you do?" Lourdes said. They kissed.

"I got here early and was walking by this hair place on Waverly and thought, 'I'm sick of the grey, my hair's too long. Why not? It'll kill some time.' Then I went shopping. Is this color too much?"

Lourdes smiled and shook her head. Javier took her hand and she didn't feel like she had in the last few years, like she was out with an uncle she was fond of. When she thinks of this night, years later, she will talk about this moment and his hair and the cranberry sweater. She will remember the rest of their date going by quickly, each moment overlapping with the next one, flashing by like the movie trailers that played that night. Some details will be vague for Lourdes, others will be very clear like the moment when the *Love Story* theme filled the theatre and the audience broke into applause. Or how the air smelled like butter and nachos. Or the very moment she was convinced she saw herself on screen, a younger self, walking on a campus where she and Javier had met. She was wearing no makeup, her pale skin smooth and tight, her own smile on screen taking her breath away. Then she heard Javier whisper, something about sisters, how they could've been sisters, she and Ali, and Lourdes was relieved that these strangers in the dark were not watching her but Ali MacGraw looking very much like Lourdes in her youth, same hair, same eyes, same body rolling around in bed with Ryan O'Neal. The whole scene made Lourdes wonder when was the last time she and Javier had made love. Five years, six, probably longer, but it wasn't her fault. "It's the pills," she had told Vinita once. "The ones that lower his blood pressure, that keep his anxiety and cholesterol in check, that keep his liver functioning. They're to blame, not me, it's them who make it difficult for him to perform, to stay alert and present. I used to try everything to get him aroused. Then I tried nothing."

"You should get yourself a lover," Javier said to her one morning. She wasn't sure if he was joking. "Maybe I will," she had said and they laughed. That was a few years ago, but his words stayed with her, taunting her, giving her, she felt, permission to explore with his blessing, free of guilt.

Ali MacGraw was dying on screen. From a hospital bed she asked Ryan O'Neal to hold her. He climbed onto her, fully clothed, and held her. Lourdes' eyes filled with tears. Javier grabbed her hand in the dark. As soon as she felt the tears on his fingers, warm and wet, Lourdes pretended to cough and pulled her hand away.

No one spoke in the cab. Javier sat at one end of the back seat looking as if he had just run a marathon. Lourdes sat at the other end counting streetlights, trying to ignore the *Love Story* theme playing in her head, insistently, each note growing louder. She kept shifting in her seat, biting her lip, scratching herself in places that didn't itch.

The cab stopped in front of the Whitney Museum and Lourdes saw colleagues entering the building. Javier said something about a grocery store, how he was going to stop at one and pick up a few things and did she need anything.

"Coffee," she said.

Last time Javier bought coffee he had it ground much finer than she liked and she was about to tell him the correct setting then changed her mind, certain he would not remember. She opened the cab door. Javier began to mumble, quietly at first, making no sense as if his sentences had shattered in his head, like glass, then reassembled themselves in random order.

The cab driver's eyes met hers in the rearview mirror. Lourdes looked away. Javier's mumbling grew louder. She pulled him close and kissed him on the lips, hard, the way she used to kiss him years ago after he had been away for days at a conference. It lasted some time, this kiss, and when it was over, Lourdes looked at Javier. His face was lit up, his head tilted to one side, his eyes staring at her.

Lourdes picked up her bag and stepped out of the cab, never looking back.

It was after 9:00 when she arrived at the house exhausted. She was not ready to go through her routine, the one that occurred every time she got home late from an evening class or school event. On these evenings Javier would always interpret her absence as an excuse to buy and drink the whiskey he wasn't supposed to drink. Her routine involved finding him drunk and passed out somewhere in the house then struggling to move him to the bed. "This is my life now," she told Vinita recently.

Lourdes removed her coat and hung it in the foyer closet. She took a quick glance around. Like every night, Javier had left all the lights on in the house; it helped him fall asleep, made him feel as though there were people in all the rooms. Lourdes turned up the heat then began drifting from room to room, turning lights off.

She reached the bedroom they had converted into a library. The room now was no longer a library but transformed, in her absence, into a classroom. The blackboard that had sat in the basement for years was now attached to a wall with large nails that further splintered the old wood frame. There was a message on the blackboard written in blue chalk: *The Napoleonic Rule of Spain and Its Consequences.* In the middle of the room sat the three school desks that had accompanied the blackboard on its journey from Puerto Rico. Javier sat in the middle desk, slumped over, his head resting on an open book in front of him, his right hand wrapped around an empty whiskey glass, a bottle of Jim Beam next to it. Lourdes shook her head, amazed, not so much by what Javier had done to the room but that he'd had the strength to do it, to drag these bulky items up the basement steps, a task that would've done her in, she was sure of it. She moved slowly by the desks, noticing the same worn book resting on each desktop, each one open to the same page, one dominated by Francisco de Goya's painting *The Second of May 1808.* She remembered the painting, having seen it for the first time years ago in Dr. Javier Ramos' history class.

Lourdes sighed. She had had a couple glasses of wine earlier at the Whitney in an attempt to relax enough to open up to her colleagues. She wasn't sure if she had the strength tonight to lift Javier, to carry him to the bedroom.

She moved the whiskey bottle and empty glass to another desk. She picked up Javier's right arm and placed it over her shoulder. *This is my life now.*

It wasn't until she had him on his feet that she realized he wasn't breathing.

# 23

For some time—or maybe for a long time—we've been following the deaf girl through Woodlawn Cemetery. I'm convinced she's lost. Or trying to walk us to death.

"How big is this place?" I say.

Luis and I are walking between headstones.

"Just over four hundred acres," he says. "Been here since 1862—no, '63."

"How do you remember this?"

"I had to when I was giving tours here. There was a test I had to take, training. Of course we didn't walk, we were on a trolley—this area looks familiar. I think Gerald is buried here. I'm going to tell Ivonne we visited him. If she calls, tell her we visited him."

The deaf girl stops suddenly and we bump into her. Luis catches her by the arm before she hits the ground. She's looking ahead. We follow her gaze. Lourdes is standing in front of Javier's headstone. We approach. Without turning around Lourdes says, "We missed her."

"How do you know?" I say.

"Vinita left these calla lilies again. They're fresh."

"How do you know they're fresh?" Luis says.

"The blooms are firm and smooth. And there's no pollen yet."

"So they were placed here...?" I say.

"A day ago. Maybe two."

The deaf girl does the sign of the cross then places a hand briefly on her father's headstone. She moves away. Luis and I do the sign of the cross. He wanders off looking at headstones. Probably searching for Gerald's.

I look at Lourdes and ask her how she's holding up. She pulls out tissues. She blows her nose. Wipes her eyes. She says, "It's been three months, but some days—like today—it feels like three days. I'm okay when I'm out of the house, when I'm teaching or doing errands. But not okay when I'm home alone."

"Have you thought of moving?"

"Every day. I just don't know what's worse. Being reminded of him or not being reminded of him."

The deaf girl comes up to us. She signs something then walks off. "I'm hungry, my daughter's hungry. Are you guys hungry?"

Lourdes does the sign of the cross, touches two fingers to Javier's headstone then starts to walk off. Luis is staring at a headstone. The deaf girl grabs his hand. They begin to walk.

I catch up to Lourdes and say, "Hey...do you remember when these two were kids and a bunch of us were at the Bronx Zoo and we forgot about them, left without them?"

Lourdes laughs and says, "I remember that, but we didn't forget about them, we just left them behind."

"Same thing."

She laughs again. "I guess it's the same thing. But we were young, Cruz, and drinking and distracted and—anyway, Vinita and I ended up finding them quickly. I don't think they were alone for more than twenty minutes, if that."

The deaf girl is now walking in front of Luis.

"And they were so young," Lourdes says. "I'm sure they don't even remember."

"Probably not."

"What made you think of that?"

"I don't know, it just...I don't know."

Luis stops to read a headstone.

Lourdes leaves my side and catches up to her daughter. Each one reaches out until they lock hands and continue walking. Neither one looks at the other.

# 24

**W**atch horses in a pasture and it won't take you long to realize they're a quiet bunch. Except for a snort or nicker here and there, they mostly live in a world of silence and wind. During my horse riding lessons, my son told me horses speak through their bodies. According to Raul, any movement—a turn of the head, a lifted leg—is their language. *They sense your emotions*, he said, *take note of your movements, your breathing, not to mention they're herd animals so they demand that another horse or human lead the herd which means when you're on a horse, it sees both of you as a herd of two and if you don't take control, if you don't lead, the horse will then run into problems.* It took me some time to grasp this concept though Ben never has. His few attempts at riding a horse have always ended with something sprained or broken. He doesn't even go near the horses anymore. Jesus is a different story. I watch him from the porch riding Bailey in the pasture with confidence and ease. Bailey trots and canters and gallops about.

I wave at workers as they climb into their vehicles and drive off. Clouds start to move in. I go to the edge of the porch and lean against a post. Bailey comes to a stop. Jesus leans forward and pats him on the neck. I wonder what's his story, this guy who knows my story well, who read me so accurately at the lake. I pace the porch replaying his words in my head. I turn and catch a glimpse of my reflection in a window and freeze, not sure what I'm looking at. I stare at myself and suddenly Jesus' assessment of me, its accuracy, is not so surprising anymore. Look at me. It doesn't take a scientist to figure out I'm miserable, that I don't belong here, that I don't care about myself, my looks. My god. I had been avoiding mirrors and I'm stunned now at how much bigger I am than I thought I was and can't believe no one has intervened. I can go to any restaurant in town and struggle to slide into a booth or sit in a chair with arms and order everything on the menu and the waiter won't say a word. Yet if I had a dozen drinks and was drunk to the bone and tried to order another drink, that same waiter would say *you've had enough* and cut me off.

Ben pulls up in his pickup truck and parks next to the BMW. I move and stand behind a wicker chair with a high back trying to hide this body I had no idea belonged to me. He steps out of the truck and walks with a limp to the porch.

What happened, Ben?

Tripped over a curb.

Are you in pain?

Lots. No chores for me this weekend.

There are workers here all week.

I know.

So why do you even have chores?

It makes me feel like I care about the place.

You can still care and pay someone to do chores.

I don't want to be that guy.

What guy?

The one who pays a sitter to raise his kid.

Right.

Want to mow the lawn this weekend?

I'd rather pay the sitter.

Bailey neighs. Ben looks out in the pasture.

Who's that?

Jesus Christ.

What?

Coghill.

Did you call them?

Not yet.

Ben limps up the porch steps and sits in the wicker chair, me behind him. He pulls out his mobile phone, pushes a number. He has Coghill on speed dial.

The line is busy.

You're injured, Ben.

So?

So let Jesus do the chores. He can use the money.

I watch Ben stand in front of Jesus as he climbs into the riding mower. Once Ben sees Jesus knows what he's doing, he limps back to the porch and sits down.

I think I'll have him paint the garage tomorrow.

I don't say anything. We sit there for a long time, side by side, like horses, nothing but silence and wind and the sound of the mower.

Later, at the dinner table, I ask Jesus to say grace. He lights up but doesn't say grace, and when I ask why, he says he's waiting for my guest. His head gestures towards the empty chair where I have set a place for the silence, finally noticed. I cover by saying I forgot that my son was away.

After grace, we chat briefly. Jesus drops a few Bible quotes. In my head, I try to guess where they're from. Ben eats, never taking his eyes off his plate. Silence takes over and carries on louder than I have ever remembered. Silverware moves, gravy pours, but we are in a silent movie now, all movement, no sound.

In the rear of the stable is a loft that the previous owner converted into a studio apartment. It has a small kitchen area and an even smaller bathroom with a shower stall. There's a window with a full-size bed under it that Jesus is standing in front of. I place a new toothbrush and toothpaste on a small table with two chairs. I turn and walk around the room, running my fingers along shelves and furniture checking for dust. I go on about fresh towels in the bathroom, a clean robe hanging on the back of the door, slippers in the closet. I hear the bathroom door close. I turn and Jesus is gone, his jeans and T-shirt are on the floor. The shower comes on. I pick up his clothes, shake them out and hang them over a chair. Something falls on the floor. A wallet. I pick it up to put it back, but I don't, I look inside. His driver's license says Joseph and a last name I can't even begin to pronounce. There's some cash. Credit cards. A photo. He's in it. Kneeling on grass. Twin teenage boys, also kneeling, next to him. An older man and woman on each side. Must be the parents because the man looks like an older version of Jesus/Joseph. Behind them there are stone stairs that, according to a sign on the left, lead to a church. Another photo of the parents. Laminated. This one is a memorial card. It shows different birth dates but the same date of death, about a month ago. Another memorial card with a photo of the twins. The date of death is the same as the parents. I'm thinking a car crash or a fire or something worse took them. I guess if you lose your whole family at once you'd want to escape, be someone else, someone like Jesus. Running around trying to save people. I guess it's either that or jump out a window.

The shower stops. I put the wallet back. There's humming in the bathroom. It's a hymn I recognize from the church-going days in my youth. The humming stops. He is whistling. Sounds like the Beatles. "Here Comes the Sun." The whistling stops.

Jesus comes out of the bathroom in a blue robe. He gives me a smile then kneels in front of the bed, does the sign of the cross, bows his head. He whispers a prayer into his hands. I think about the photos in his wallet. I want to say something, console him in some way but can't figure out how to do that without him knowing I was snooping. Maybe I'll pretend to read him the way he read me at the lake, like a Wikipedia entry, say generic things like *You look sad, miserable, distant.* And why stop there, why not add *You look like you're grieving,* then maybe he'll open up. Or maybe I just need to keep my mouth shut.

Jesus does the sign of the cross. He removes the robe, tosses it aside. Naked, he slips into bed, turns his back to me like I have already left the room. Suddenly I'm overwhelmed with sadness, my hand going across my eyes, wiping tears that haven't even arrived. I turn off the light and leave.

Ben stirs in his sleep next to me. My eyes trace the cracks in the ceiling. I think about how I will wander the rest of my life on a farm in a town so inconsequential, so dreary that I refuse to recall its name.

I get out of bed.

In the dark, I get dress quietly. I think about packing a suitcase, grabbing my favorite items, when I realize I have no favorite items. It's all replaceable. I go find my purse. I leave the house. I tiptoe down the porch steps and climb into the BMW, close the door quietly. I put the key in the ignition and I'm about to turn it then stop. I look through the windshield. I stare at the stable.

I walk across the lawn towards the stable, my path lit by moonlight. The sliding door on the stable has been left open so that the cool evening air prevents the horses from overheating. The moonlight leaves me when I enter the stable, only to reappear at the opening at the other end. A horse grunts in a stall. In the dark I climb the stairs to the loft apartment, the banister guiding me. I open the door. Moonlight sneaks in through open blinds. Jesus is asleep. I listen to his breathing. Then I wake him.

Sometime later, in the BMV, I fidget with the broken radio as I drive in the dark. Jesus sits next to me.

You aren't swayed by men, he says.

*You aren't swayed by men.*

Because you pay no attention to who they are, he says.

*The Gospel According to Mark.*

I smile and put my hand on his. It is wet.

There's tissue in the glove box, I say.

What?

Your hand is wet.

I turn on the interior car light and stop the car. I pull off the road, look at Jesus. His lap is covered in blood. He holds out his hands. There, in his palms, are holes with blood pouring from them, a bloody switchblade on his lap. I say something, I'm sure of it.

It's okay, he says.

Then I say something else.

It doesn't hurt.

Jesus looks out the window and begins to whistle softly. The Beatles. "Yesterday."

We sit there until he goes through three, maybe four Beatles songs. He pulls his legs up until his feet are on the seat. He wraps his arms around his legs. I open the glovebox, pull out tissues and wipe the blood away, thinking about how far away Coghill is, what streets to take, where to turn.

He says, I miss them.

I think about the photos in his wallet.

My family, I miss them.

I finish wiping the blood, grateful that the holes were only deep pricks. I bunch up tissues into a ball and tell him to press his palms against it and don't let go. I toss the switchblade out the window. He doesn't say a word, seems relieved. I turn off the interior light, start the car. Not a headlight in sight. I drive until I come to an intersection and stop.

I think it's that way, he says.

Hmm?

Coghill.

He begins to sing another Beatles song, the joy in his voice pierces through me. I look in the rearview mirror and see them, my brown eyes, and they aren't sad or lifeless, they're alive and beautiful and I say, Ever been to the Bronx?

# 25

At first glance, the desk appeared to be made of some exotic wood, something from a foreign country, very expensive, solid all the way through. But it was just a birch veneer hiding man-made garbage underneath. This was the desk I sat at, years ago, telling loan applicants they could afford a home I knew they couldn't. *Luis, are you sure we can afford this? Of course I'm sure.* I wasn't comfortable doing this, this telling of lies to people, first-time buyers mostly. But I had to if I was going to hit my sales goals, something that became easy to do once the housing market went insane, so insane that me and my colleagues didn't have time to take care of minor details like verifying borrowers' income or looking the other way when we came across applicants with not the best credit, pushing everything and everyone through on questionable mortgages that no one questioned until the housing market crashed and, well, that was the end of that. After that I rarely sat at my desk. My final days on the job were spent picking up keys in abandoned homes. My last day played out like this: For the third time this week I'm in an empty house wandering from room to room, listening to the floors creak, imagining where the furniture once stood when there are no clues like imprints in the carpet when there is no carpet, like this house, wood floors in every room. Except for the faint sound of traffic coming through the windows, it is quiet. My colleagues dread this part of the job—roaming abandoned homes in search of keys. They say it reminds them of how they failed these families. I find an empty home comforting. Peaceful. I'd lie on the floor and rest if there was carpeting but not today. I stand there, eyes closed for some time until I'm disturbed by signs from a dead person which I ignore and that's followed by a commotion on the street, screeching tires, car horns, people swearing. I continue roaming the place. This home is the cleanest one I've been in all month. Usually the home is left a mess, shit everywhere, the kind of stuff that lets you know how this chapter ended for these homeowners, like blood-stained hospital beds, oxygen tanks, unpaid bills, collection-agency notices, things you don't want to see like sex toys and dirty underwear. Then there are the nasty odors like rotting food and animal feces and all kinds of unidentifiable smells. But not this home. This one smells like it was scrubbed from top to bottom with Clorox and Mr. Clean and, so far, it appears as if they've left nothing behind. These owners were first-time buyers. *We're so tired of renting, Luis, help us, would you, help us get this house. Of course I'll help you.* A nice couple with two teenage boys. Accustomed to years of living in rentals, always in the habit of leaving them like this place, clean and in order, to ensure the full return of their security deposit. I go into the kitchen. Yellow cabinets, burgundy walls, like a café in Italy I saw in a movie once without the charm. The appliances are gone, but everything else seems in order. Some owners feel they have to destroy the place to make it harder for us to resell. They rip everything out. Cabinets, counters, doors, for starters. However the most popular trick with owners these days is to pour cement down the sinks so all the plumbing has to be re-done, so that so much money is spent repairing pipes we couldn't possibly make a profit. I turn on the faucet and let the water run until I'm convinced the pipes are fine. The home is freezing, but I open a window to let out the fumes left behind by Clorox and Mr. Clean. I look out onto the street.

Things are quiet again. I take a deep breath and exhale, over and over, and I want to crawl into a ball and sleep for the rest of the day, but work must be done. Keys are on the kitchen counter sitting on a note with two words, the same two words all month—*fuck you*—as if all my former clients got together and elected to use the same two words as a clue, like serial killers, to let me know it was them. I look at the two words and it hurts. Not because of the harsh words they chose but the lack of punctuation like I wasn't worth the emotion an exclamation point would hint at. I wish they'd at least placed a period after *fuck you* because that would've told me this brief sentence—floating on all that white space—has ended and there would be no more sentences to come, this story is over, let's all move on. By not using any punctuation, the two words appear open-ended as if they're on a loop. Two words that for the last month have been constantly appearing before me like a pair of flies you can't get rid of no matter how hard you swat at them. I shove the note and keys into my pocket and walk into the living room. Peach walls. A hole in a wall with half a baseball bat sticking out from it, the other half on the floor. The older son probably. *Luis come to Junior's baseball game this weekend, he wants to thank you, he's never had his own room before. I'd love to.* I stare at the hole. It appears spontaneous. I suspect they were all in the car ready to pull away and Junior remembered he left his bat behind. He runs inside and searches until he finds the bat in the back of a closet then was suddenly overwhelmed with emotion, enraged he was going to have to share a room again with his little brother, a thought that got the best of him and he just started swinging the bat.

Definitely not premeditated. I look up. A spray-painted message in black on the beige ceiling: *Once upon a time there was love here until there wasn't.* Like I've done for the past month in every home I've picked up keys in, I tell myself this vandalism was caused by neighborhood kids even though there are no signs of a break-in. I look at the two windows in the center wall.

Worn, ivory shades are rolled up. I walk up to a window and pull down the shade. It comes off its track and hits me on the head and I start crying like a child then acting like one, kicking base boards, shaking my fists at the ceiling, saying things like *You did this, Luis, you destroyed this family.* Ten minutes later I'm lying on the wood floor, in tears, my head against my coat now rolled up into a ball. I want to look away from the ceiling but can't. *Once upon a time there was love here until there wasn't.* I think about going home and writing the same message on my ceilings as well as the walls and mirrors and anywhere else my girlfriend Ginger would see it. We both keep threatening to leave, both know it's over, but neither one of us can follow through on anything, the only thing we have in common anymore. I get up off the floor and put on my coat. In the bathroom I look around. White tiles, lavender walls. I open the faucet, let the water run, all's well here. There's no shower curtain. The lid on the toilet bowl is up. The room is empty except for the toilet paper. I tear some paper off the roll, blow my nose, wipe my eyes, toss the paper towards the toilet bowl. The paper hits the wall and falls behind the bowl. I shake my head. In the hallway, I yell, again shaking my fists at the world as if the world had anything to do with this, as if the world forced me to lie to these people. *Luis, my husband and I are concerned about this high interest rate and stipulations, why so many stipulations, is it because of our credit? Yes, but don't focus on that, focus on your dream of owning a home.* I think about the paper I threw behind the toilet just lying there collecting bacteria. I return to the bathroom and reach behind the toilet bowl, searching for the paper and I hit something that's not the paper. An empty pill bottle rolls out. I close my eyes. Nausea kicks in. I run cold water, splash it on my face and sit on the edge of the tub until my stomach settles. I exit the bathroom and stand in the hallway. Green walls. I move on. The first bedroom is red, the second turquoise, the third lavender. Something about all these colors begins to scratch hard at my nerves. Something desperate, contrived, juvenile, as if the colors were chosen by a child with his first box of crayons, one determined to use every color in the box just because he could. Months ago when I picked up the first set of keys in an abandoned home, I was optimistic. My company had the home cleaned, painted, staged then put back on the market and, months later, it still sits empty along with all the other abandoned homes without a single offer on any of them despite multiple price reductions. I'm not optimistic anymore. My company will no longer pay to have these empty homes prepped for the market. Look at this one. It will take lots of work and money to remove all this color, to depersonalize it with something neutral like white or close to it that makes it easy for prospective buyers to imagine the space as their own, a blank canvas. And it will take more work and money my company refuses to spend to stage the home, but you *have* to stage it because buyers' heads are filled with so many hopes and fears that there's no room left to imagine where to place a goddamn sofa. I go back to the living room and stare at the message on the ceiling, thinking about these owners, how I called him and his wife repeatedly trying to work something out. I wanted this to work out for them, I mean, it wasn't their fault, no one could've predicted they'd both lose their jobs in the same week. Christ. It wasn't like I was sitting at my desk handing out loans then wishing these people's lives collapsed. I'm not in the real estate business. I didn't want their home. *Hey, it's Luis calling again, I know unemployment is not much, but we can work something out, keep you in your home, call me.* But this couple never called. Never made an attempt to work with me. It was almost as if they were glad this happened, thrilled to go out from under their ridiculous mortgage payment and return to the comforts of a reasonably priced rental. And where do these people go now with this failure on their back like a scarlet letter? They couldn't possibly qualify for a lease now. Are they depending on family and friends, living on their sofas and guestrooms, storing their stuff in their attics and basements? That is what I think about every night while trying to sleep on the sofa as Ginger sleeps in our bed after the fighting ends and the television has long been shut off and it's past 3:00 in the morning and I feel more alone with Ginger around than when I'm alone. Like right now in this empty house. I take one last look around, opening and closing closet doors. I look at my watch. I should go home but don't want to. Maybe I'll go back to the office, sit among the chaos and clutter of my desk. I go out the front door. As the keys rattle in my hand, I decide this is it, no more, no more picking up keys in empty homes. You can't make this right, find something else to do. Flip burgers, scrub toilets, park cars, *anything*.

An hour later I'm shopping with my own money then return with gallons of paints and brushes and rollers and paint every room white. *Hi Luis, we just unpacked the last box, we still can't believe you made this happen for us, the boys love their rooms, thanks a mil!*

# 26

A pigeon lands on the hood of the Granada. I stare at it while I wait for a traffic light to change. The pigeon is blue and grey or bluish grey. Two black bands on the wing. A black tip on the tail. The eyes are red. So are the feet with their three toes and white claws digging into the Granada's finish I recently had polished. As the pigeon moves its head, the feathers on its neck change colors. Grey to green to lavender then back to grey. It turns its head and looks at me with one red eye. The traffic light changes to green. The Granada moves, the pigeon flies off.

On Valentine Avenue I turn and park near Luis' apartment building. Clouds move in giving us a break from the blinding sun. The four of us step out of the Granada dripping in sweat. No one is talking, but there's a conversation going on in signs about climate change between Luis and the deaf girl with Lourdes interjecting here and there. Luis brings up something he saw on the news about our water, that it's not secure and this worries him and sometimes he gets up in the middle of the night and turns on faucets to make sure there's still water in the world. The deaf girl rolls her eyes at Luis as we enter his apartment. She goes into the bathroom. Lourdes sits at the dining table with a small paper bag from the Puerto Rican restaurant we just ate at. She opens the bag, pulls out a to-go container, plastic spoons, napkins, sets them on the table. She opens the container. Two pieces of flan sit side by side.

"Luis, bring me some birthday candles," Lourdes says.

"I don't have any."

"Everyone has birthday candles. They just forget they have them."

"I don't."

"Go check your junk drawer."

"I don't have a junk drawer."

"Everyone has a junk drawer."

"If it's junk, it's going in the garbage, not a drawer."

"Luis, *please.*"

Luis goes into the kitchen. We hear drawers opening and closing.

I look at Lourdes and mouth *I'm sorry.* She waves me off and says, "He was like that when I used to babysit him. I'd tell him to go take a shower and he'd say stuff like, 'No point in wasting water if I'm just going to get dirty tomorrow.' It was always a twenty-minute debate to get him to do anything."

"Well, don't take it personally. He was like that with us. With everyone. I think he'd be further along in life if he'd learn how to shut up."

"Now Ivonne challenged me as a child but not as bad as Luis. And Olivia was always so quiet with her reading and writing that I'd forget she was around. I called her yesterday, Olivia. Wanted to see how's the teaching going."

"She says she likes it."

"She *says* that, but her heart's not in it. All she talked about was the time off for the holidays, for the whole summer—not once mentioning the students."

"I spoke to her briefly last week. She sounds happy."

"That's because she's seeing a theatre professor."

"Those online things never work out for her."

"No, no, no, she met him on campus. They've gone out a few times, mostly to see plays. She loves plays now, she says, planning on writing one."

A drawer is slammed shut in the kitchen. The deaf girl returns as Luis appears and says, "No candles, but I found a box of matches." She looks at the box and signs.

*birthday candles*

Luis shakes his head and holds out the box of matches. She takes the box from him and pulls out a wooden match. She lights it and inserts it upright on a flan. Lourdes begins to sing "Happy Birthday" while the deaf girl signs along. Luis and I join in. Everyone is singing in a different key. It's not a pleasant sound. Luis blows out the match. We clap. We each pick up a spoon and start digging into the flans.

The telephone rings.

Luis answers the cordless nearby and disappears with it into the bedroom. The rest of us finish off the flans. Wipe our mouths with napkins. Lourdes places everything back in the bag. The deaf girl takes the bag into the kitchen. We hear water running.

"Where's Ginger?" Lourdes says. "Is she still in the picture?"

I shrug.

Lourdes points to the floor and whispers, "Check those clothes. See if there's anything of hers in there."

There are piles of clothes in the living room like Luis was sorting his laundry and got distracted. I can't tell if they're clean or not. I move from pile to pile digging through each one with the edge of my foot.

"It's all his," I say.

I look around. My son has lived here for four years and this is the fifth or sixth time I've stood in his apartment. Each visit revealing a surprise. A new chair or lamp or piece of artwork.

I see nothing new today except two birthday cards on top of the television. A framed photo hanging over it. I'm surprised because this photo is one Vinita has spent weeks searching for, accusing everyone, including Luis, of stealing it. He denied taking it yet here it is in plain sight.

A black-and-white photo of his mother and Grace Kelly.

"I hope Ginger is gone," Lourdes says.

The framed photo has fingerprints on the glass. I wipe them off with the edge of my T-shirt. I stare at this photo taken a lifetime ago when Vinita spent her days chasing her dream while I altered costumes in the costume department at Paramount Studios.

Lourdes picks up a shirt off the floor. She inspects it, smells it. She does this to a couple of pieces of clothing. Once she's convinced everything is clean, she starts folding clothes. I look at the photo on the wall. I try to remember the name of the guy who got me the job at Paramount. He was also a seamstress I had worked with. A young Italian from the Bronx who moved to California after one too many brutal winters. Stefano, I think his name was.

The deaf girl enters from the kitchen. She looks at her mother then starts folding clothes with her. In the bedroom Luis laughs on the telephone.

I look back at the photo. 1953.

Vinita began to be intrigued by Grace after seeing her in televised plays. The being intrigued turn into admiration after we saw her in *Mogambo* at Grauman's Chinese Theatre on Hollywood Boulevard. Not only did Vinita admire Grace's performances but how the actress was able to maintain the flawless figure Vinita once had, the one she was struggling to get back, but I didn't know what she was talking about, Vinita looked amazing, I told her all the time, and thin but not thin enough, she'd say, waving a piece a paper with her old measurements on it. One day I arrived at our small apartment off of Gower and found Vinita in tears. It was a rough day, she said, something about Olivia in her crib crying for hours, something about her body refusing to shed weight despite her eating like a bird and why can't I look like that again, pointing to a photo of Grace Kelly in the newspaper, and when I told her Grace was filming at the studio, Vinita perked up, asked if I could sneak her onto the lot. When I told her no, Vinita's face collapsed and I felt bad and that's when Olivia started crying in the other room. Vinita stood up, but instead of heading towards Olivia, she left the apartment. The next morning at the studio, I was asked by my supervisor to pick up a costume at Grace's trailer that afternoon. I immediately called Vinita and that afternoon I snuck her onto the lot. Had her pretend she was my assistant. Told her to stand behind me and don't say a word. Vinita followed me with my clipboard in her hand to Sound Stage 6 until we arrived at Grace's trailer. I knocked on the door. It swung open and an older woman with grey hair stood there. We exchanged words and the woman vanished inside, then Grace appeared in a black dress with a fitted bodice, pearl earrings and a three-layer pearl necklace, looking more beautiful in person than on the screen at Grauman's Chinese Theatre. Behind me I heard Vinita gasp while Grace and I exchanged words about a dress she could move in but was too tight in the waist to climb the fire escape she had been going up and down yesterday during rehearsals, leaving her breathless. A sleeveless ivory dress embroidered with copper-colored flowers that suddenly appeared out of the trailer on a hanger in the hand of the woman with grey hair who handed me the dress then disappeared. And that's when Vinita spoke to Grace. *How do you do it? Keep your waist so small?* And before I knew it, the two of them were carrying on about diets while I'm throwing Vinita a look that said something like what part of *Do not say a word* didn't you understand. Then Vinita said her weight has been a challenge since she had a baby, and when Grace heard the word *baby*, she choked up. Her eyes brimmed with tears. Grace congratulated Vinita who reached into a pocket and pulled out the Kodak Brownie camera I'd given her and asked Grace if she would take a picture with her and my heart stopped and I said *No* louder than I wanted to. I fell silent as crew members walked by then told Vinita that the taking of photos on the lot is prohibited. Grace smiled and whispered *I won't tell* and she took the camera from Vinita and handed it to me and we moved to the side of the trailer, out of view from everyone, and the picture was taken and Grace didn't tell, but someone did because, by the end of the week, I was fired for taking a photo that now hangs in my son's apartment over an old television.

I stare at the photo. In the glass' reflection, Lourdes appears. She says, "My god I haven't seen this in years."

I stand there and wonder about that time. That place. How I wanted to leave. How Vinita wanted to stay. Neither one of us knew what to do with a baby. Poor Olivia. One day Vinita said, "Lourdes would know what to do. Let's go back to the Bronx. Just for a little while."

I move closer to the photo. The frame is crooked. I straighten it.

Luis returns with the cordless and places it in its cradle.

"That was Ivonne wishing me *Happy Birthday*," he says and signs.

"How are things on the farm?"

"Raul went to Puerto Rico to be with some guy. And she left Ben."

No one looks surprised. Lourdes inspects her nails, her daughter yawns. I pick up a T-shirt off the floor and hang it over a chair. Luis moves to the table, looks around. "She's driving here now. Should be in the city in an hour or so. She was calling from a rest stop, rambling like she always does, not making a lot of sense and it sounds like she went back to church, kept talking about Jesus and Jesus is with her and—what happened to my flan?"

# 27

Before her husband's death, Dolores spent her days consumed with housework and caring for Vinita and Lourdes while their father ran the coffee plantation, taking on multiple roles in an effort to increase dwindling profits. Dolores moved about like a mouse, barely raising her voice above a whisper so as not to disturb her husband who was always sleeping or working in his office in the rear of the house. Upon his death Dolores hired a foreman and a bookkeeper then took the money she had received from her husband's life insurance policy and bought the land next door to expand the coffee plantation. Within two years, profits tripled. Dolores redecorated the house. She replaced her cheap and dowdy wardrobe with the latest fashions from the States.

And while Lourdes sat in her room doing schoolwork, Vinita watched as women came to the house to do her mother's hair or show her how to apply makeup or what shoes to wear with what. It didn't take long for Dolores to lose interest in housework and seeing to her daughters' needs; a sudden change that didn't go unnoticed by the sisters, now in their teens. Every night, as they prepared for bed, Vinita would try to convince Lourdes that their mother—the attentive woman who was always there for them—would return soon. She was absolutely certain of this, as if their mother were a misplaced dress that would reappear any day now in the back of a closet.

But the mother they once knew never returned. The new Dolores always looked like someone on their way to a lavish party with her opulent jewelry and fitted dresses made of the finest fabrics. Never a hair out of place. The subtle makeup enhancing what was already beautiful. At times she played music at full volume while her voice and laughter echoed loudly throughout the house. She finally got the German Shepherds she had always wanted, the ones her husband would never let her have. Then she hired a live-in housekeeper to cook and clean and take care of her daughters who, over time, saw their mother maybe once or twice a week when she was able to make it to the dinner table, often with a guest or two: neighbors, workers, suitors. And in the summer, late at night, after one too many shots of whiskey, Dolores would wake her daughters and give them hugs and kisses and drag them out of bed and they'd laugh and run in the coffee fields with the dogs chasing them the whole time. Then they'd stop to catch their breath and Vinita and Lourdes would follow their mother back to the house as the *coquíes* sang around them. And it was these midnight walks in the coffee fields that played in Vinita's head now in slow motion as her children walked behind her. They stopped walking and waited for a traffic light to change underneath the 3rd Avenue El train in the Bronx. Vinita looked at the snow on the ground and sighed. She stood there holding a blue suitcase with eleven-year-old Olivia on one side, nine-year-old Ivonne on the other holding her brother Luis' hand, the boy four.

"We used to live up there," Ivonne said.

She was pointing out a building to Luis in front of the El train while explaining how the windows would shake every time a train went by.

The traffic light turned green.

"Let's go," Olivia said.

They followed Vinita in the snow along Tremont Avenue, onto a side street, through the entrance of Serrano Funeral Home, down a long corridor with burgundy carpeting filled with golden light spilling from overhead light fixtures made of square frosted glass, past a viewing room with an older woman wiping down folding chairs, her grey hair tied in a bun. The children didn't look around with an exploring gaze the way children do when they enter a new space. They had done this march behind their mother here many times.

They turned a corner and stopped in front of a wooden door painted a deep red.

Vinita turned to them and said, "I'll be back as soon as I can."

"Where are you going, Mami?" Luis said.

"Hollywood."

The sisters rolled their eyes as they removed their gloves in unison.

"I left a note for your father to pick you up when he gets home from work." Vinita opened the red door and led them inside. Mr. Serrano greeted them with a smile from the other side of the room. He was applying makeup to a female corpse in a yellow dress lying on a mortuary table with wheels. He went over to Vinita and they hugged. They spoke briefly in Spanish. Vinita kissed her children then left with her suitcase through the red door.

Mr. Serrano smiled at the children and said, "Who wants to make a quarter?"

The children raised their hands.

"Olivia, you do the nails this time," he said. "Ivonne you do the jewelry and Luis put on her shoes." Without hesitation the children went to work, more confident and relaxed than when they first took on these tasks over a year ago. None of them shook or closed their eyes anymore when a hand brushed against the cold skin of the dead. Now they handled the corpse gently with a casual ease. They enjoyed Mr. Serrano's company, his laughter, the snacks he gave them whenever a body first arrived. Snacks that had to be eaten on the other side of the red door. Not because Mr. Serrano didn't want crumbs on the dead but because he didn't feel it was appropriate for them, at such a young age, to witness the embalming process.

"We have to hurry," Mr. Serrano said. "We got Mr. Marino coming in soon. By the way, I have cookies for you guys today. I thought of bringing in some flan and I did but it, uh, disappeared..." He tapped his big belly and they all laughed.

Vinita was back out in the snow on Tremont Avenue, climbing into a taxi as the driver placed her blue suitcase into the trunk. In the back seat she closed her eyes and slept, and when she awoke, she was getting off a bus at Tremont and 3rd Avenue, blinded by sunlight that was no longer blocked by the 3rd Avenue El, the whole thing demolished over thirty years ago.

Vinita crossed the street and walked until she arrived at Serrano Funeral Home, making her way down the corridor now covered in dark green carpeting, fluorescent lighting above. She came to the red door, stopped and looked around, seeing her children for a second, suddenly wondering how a woman who wanted no children ended up with three, especially since the first one was so hard on her, she had told her mother. Dolores advised Vinita to have another child right away because, if she didn't, Olivia was going to run her into the ground. But Vinita was adamant she was never going to have any more children to which her mother said in Spanish, "If you get one dog, it will follow you around all day for years and you'll never have a moment to yourself. But if you get a second, even a third dog, they will chase each other all day long and leave you alone so you can breathe."

And with that Ivonne was born.

Vinita opened the red door and entered the room. Lourdes was standing in front of the mortuary table where Javier lay in a dark blue suit, white shirt, red-and-blue paisley tie. Mr. Serrano's oldest son, Mateo, was standing at the head of the table.

"I don't like the hair parted to the side," Lourdes said.

"But that's how he always wore it," Mateo said. "And the way he wore it in the pictures you gave me."

They turned to Vinita, acknowledged her with a nod then returned their focus to Javier.

"I always wanted him to wear his hair back," Lourdes said. She stared at Javier for a few seconds. "Let's comb it back."

Mateo began combing Javier's hair back. Vinita removed her gloves as she walked over to Lourdes.

"Mami doesn't think she can make it," Vinita whispered.

"Why not?"

"She's eighty-six. Traveling is hard for her."

Lourdes bit her lip.

"How's that?" Mateo said.

Javier's hair was combed back. Lourdes nodded and looked at her sister. Vinita disapproved with a raised eyebrow then, out of nowhere, felt uncomfortable as though she had walked in on an intimate moment between a woman and her husband.

Vinita had nowhere to be, but she said she had to leave.

"You just got here," Lourdes said.

"I forgot I have to pick something up."

Vinita kissed Lourdes on the cheek, gave Mateo a nod. On her way out the red door, she heard Lourdes say, "Let's part his hair the way it was."

Vinita walked down the corridor. She stopped in front of a viewing room to put on her gloves. She looked inside. Mateo's twin teenage boys were in the room. One of them was straightening out folding chairs while the other wiped them down with a cloth. The room was empty and then it was not, every chair suddenly filled with Lourdes and Vinita's family and friends while Javier lay in an open casket at the front of the room, former students scattered about.

The deaf girl stood in front of her father, a hand lying on his arm. Lourdes sat in the front row with Vinita next to her.

Luis was in the back row when Olivia arrived and sat next to him. They kissed and Luis whispered, "Where have you been?"

"Between writing and teaching...Don't ask." She looked around the room. "I don't know half these people."

The deaf girl walked away from her father and sat down. An older couple went up to the casket arm in arm. The woman began to wail. If the man had not held her up, she would have collapsed to the floor. Luis leaned into Olivia and whispered, "That's Javier's sister from Florida."

"Have I ever met her?"

"Many times."

"I don't remember her."

"Poor Olivia. It won't be long now."

"Stop. Where's Ivonne and her clan?"

"She didn't want to come here."

"I think she's done with the Bronx."

"No, *here*, to this place. She told Aunt Lourdes to have the funeral somewhere else because she didn't want to come in *here,* says she still has nightmares about this place. I don't. Do you?"

Olivia shook her head. "This place was a blessing. I have a lot of issues, but fear of death is not one of them. Where's our father?"

"On his way, I guess."

They watched Lourdes as she went up to the casket.

"Last week I was sitting in my apartment," Luis said, "and Javier appeared in front of me. He was bouncing a red ball. After a few seconds, the ball froze in mid-air then fell to the ground. That's my sign for a person's heart stopped. And at that very moment, when the ball hit the floor, the phone rang and it was Papi telling me Javier just died and I told him 'I know. Javier told me his heart stopped.'"

"What did Papi say?"

"He hung up on me."

Cruz appeared with a tan suitcase. Behind him, walking with the aid of a cane, Dolores followed. Cruz went to take her arm and she pulled it away and kept walking then nodded at Luis and Olivia when she passed them. When she arrived at the front of the room, a surprised Vinita hugged her while the deaf girl kissed her grandmother on the cheek. The old woman handed her cane to Vinita then walked towards the casket slowly. Lourdes felt a hand on her arm and turned her head, and when she saw Dolores, she squeezed her eyes tight shut. It wasn't until her mother whispered *Está bien* that Lourdes covered her face with her hands and wept.

Vinita watched them from her chair, her mind wandering somewhere else; the house in Puerto Rico, their room as girls, the window with the white lace sheers, the coffee fields, her father and mother walking through them in the moonlight arm in arm, the glow of his burning cigarette following them like a firefly, and the songs of the *coquíes* echoing through her mother's tidy rooms.

# 28

The woman with the blue suitcase.

She walks a street that is unfamiliar to her.

Her eyes jump from one storefront window to another.

A pizzeria. A discount store. A bodega.

All places she has been in many times.

She is being followed by a headache she can't shake.

A bottle of water is purchased, aspirins is taken.

The walk continues.

At a traffic light, she wipes sweat off her face.

A corner is turned and everything changes, everything is familiar.

She walks and waves at passersby who call her name.

A conversation with an old man ends as quickly as it begins.

The headache subsides, another corner is turned.

A street lined with houses.

From an open window Celia Cruz is heard singing.

The woman walks until she sees it, the house she's been looking for.

She starts to cross the street then stops.

In the air she smells *sofrito* like the one she used to make for her family.

She closes her eyes, inhales and listens to Celia's voice.
The woman with the blue suitcase exhales and crosses the street.

# 29

Then Ivonne arrives with a man named Jesus.

After introductions they collapse on Luis' sofa next to the deaf girl while Lourdes and I sit across from them. Luis hands them bottles of water. Ivonne says nothing, just gulps the water down. Jesus says thank you half a dozen times like he was given a bottle of thirty-year-old whiskey.

"Drove eight hours straight," Ivonne says, "only stopping for food and potty breaks." Small talk takes place, trivial stuff.

No one asks about the bandages around Jesus' hands or what happened to Ivonne because I don't recognize the Ivonne that sits in front of me. This is not the Ivonne who left the Bronx a couple of years ago with a small waist. This Ivonne is bigger than I've ever seen her. And she looks exhausted like she's been doing everything on the farm herself.

Yet despite her exhaustion, Ivonne is more polite than usual. The curtness she sets aside for her family is nowhere to be found. Maybe living on a farm has changed her. Or maybe she's being pleasant to us because she has a guest sitting next to her, this Jesus fellow with the good manners. Seems very sincere when he asks each of us what we do for a living while looking us in the eyes so intensely you're afraid to look away. When he gets to Lourdes, he goes on about the importance of shaping minds through teaching then carries on about Socrates for some time. With me he goes on about the first dress called the Tarkhan Dress discovered in an Egyptian tomb that was over five thousand years old. When he gets to the deaf girl, he signs to her and I am surprised and not surprised. He goes on about diamonds and asks the deaf girl if she knew that some of the first diamonds ever found were in India in the fourth century. He describes these early diamonds in vivid details like they were right in front of him. It's Luis' turn and he tells Jesus he does a little of this and that and a lot of worrying about the lack of water in the world and the environment. Jesus mentions a writer, Rachel Carson, a book, *Silent Spring*, how it disturbed him and yes, Luis says, I read it and they carry on about a storybook opening that draws you in with a romantic view of nature that is eventually destroyed by pesticides and the sound of birds is no more and please tell me, Luis says to Ivonne, that you don't use pesticides on the farm, that you can still hear the birds. My daughter yawns and goes into the kitchen and the conversation returns to trivial stuff like extreme temperatures and Lourdes shares that, when she first arrived in the city, years ago, the summers were so mild compared to now and this sets Luis off and he starts talking about climate change with Jesus until the deaf girl interrupts with her hands, signing about death and her father and that's when I've had enough.

In the kitchen I ask Ivonne how long she's in town for.

"I'm not going back," she says.

"Ben called looking for you."

"What did he say?"

"That he's looking for you. And that people from Coghill—whatever that is—came looking for Jesus, but he'd already left. So is this guy in there going to be husband number six?"

"No, he's just someone I'm helping out. His family is gone."

"On vacation?"

"They're dead. He's struggling."

"And what are you planning to do with this Jesus guy?"

"His name is Joseph."

"I heard Jesus."

"I said Jesus, but his name is Joseph, but call him Jesus."

"You're talking in circles. Have you been drinking?"

"He's pretending he's Jesus Christ. That's what he's gotta do. Everyone grieves differently."

"Gotta?"

"That's what he *has to* do."

"Well, he's very smart."

"What? That little show in there?"

I nod. "He knows a lot about everything."

"He knows nothing, just has a lot of stuff memorized."

"I was impressed."

"Don't be. He told me in the car that, a few years ago, he was on *Jeopardy* after spending a year memorizing facts about every subject he could think of. He drove me nuts in the car. Everything he saw out the window triggered a release of these *facts*. A billboard sign, an old car, a rainbow, trees. He can't seem to shut it off—anyway, what's going on with Mami? Any sign of her?" She picks up a box of crackers on the counter, inspecting all sides of it, searching for something, the expiration date, I suspect.

"We found flowers she left at Javier's headstone."

"Calla lilies."

"Calla lilies."

"She's always loved calla lilies." Ivonne opens the box of crackers. "And doing her Katharine Hepburn impression from that movie."

As she eats a cracker, Ivonne becomes Katharine Hepburn, mimicking her voice, speaking casually until she chokes up with emotion. "'Hello, Mother...The calla lilies are in bloom again...Such a strange flower...suitable to any occasion...I carried them on my wedding day and...now I place them here in...in...?'"

"'In memory of something that has died.'"

Ivonne wipes tears away then suddenly laughs loudly. Someone in the other room shushes her. "Apparently I'm disturbing The Jesus Show."

She puts the box of crackers down, opens the bottom of the re-frigerator. After a few seconds, she shakes her head and closes it then opens the top freezer and shakes her head some more. "Not only is it frost free, it's food free. No wonder he's always so damn trim. My brother's onto something here. I mean, it's the perfect diet. Don't keep food around." She closes the freezer and starts opening cabinet doors. "And why are you even looking for Mami? She always comes back now. It's not like when we were kids and she'd disappear to California and you had to go get her and you'd leave us with Uncle Javier and Aunt Lourdes." She looks over her shoulder then whispers, "Poor Aunt Lourdes, she tried. I love her, but she was as bad of a mother as my mother. Of course, I'm not much better—okay, Papi, get that look off your face."

"What look?"

"The look you always get when we talk about Mami in not a nice way. Next you're going to start with the clichés. Saying stuff like 'She did the best she could.'" She turns around and opens another cabinet door.

"She did."

"I hope that was not her best—oh my god, Luis!" She is looking inside a cabinet. "He has dishes everywhere! *Everywhere!* And nothing to put on them. What the fuck?"

"Ivonne!"

"Sorry."

"I'm going home."

"Don't go. It's still early. I was going to order food for us."

"I'm tired. I need to get to bed and get up early and continue the search."

"Oh stop. I'm sure Mami's at some hotel nearby sleeping or out see-ing a movie. Once she clears her head, she'll be back. And stop acting like you're put out when she goes away. We all know it's the search you enjoy."

"I don't enjoy it."

"You love it. The search has always been your excuse to get out, see the family, spend time with Luis."

"Oh Luis." I sigh. "You know I invite him over all the time or offer to take him out to eat or see a movie and he always says no, says he's busy, but he's never busy when I ask him to search for his mother. He always makes time for that."

"Is Ginger still in the picture?"

"I don't know and I'm afraid to ask. I ask one thing, Luis hears something else. I say, 'How are you, Luis?', he hears 'What the fuck are you doing with your life, loser?' Then he gets loud, defensive, the hands all over the place—anyway I hope Ginger's in the picture. I hope anyone is in the picture—And what is this all about?!" I'm waving a finger back and force across Ivonne's new body.

She places a hand on her large belly then gently rubs it, the way she used to when she was pregnant. "You know I'll get back in shape."

"You always do. I just don't understand why you allow yourself to get to this place—" There is clapping in the other room.

Ivonne goes to the kitchen doorway and looks in the living room.

"What's going on?" I say.

"They're playing a game. Come on."

In the living room we're playing something like *Jeopardy*.

There's only one category: Bible Quotes.

The host: Jesus Christ.

The contestants: a bunch of lost Catholics.

He's giving clues.

We're calling out answers.

Hands are signing in the air.

You can't tell who's saying what.

It's going something like this:


'Be very careful then how you live, not as unwise but as wise.'

What is *Ephesians*?

'I have no greater joy than to hear that my children are walking in the truth.'

What is the *Book of Luke*?

Incorrect.

What is the *Book of John*?

'What good is it for you to gain the whole world yet forfeit your soul?'

Who is Ivonne Santana? Ha ha.

*what is the book of mark?*

'A time to be born
a time to die—'

What is "There is a Season"?

Incorrect.

Finish the clue.

'A time to plant
a time to uproot
a time to kill
a time to heal—'

What is "Turn! Turn! Turn!"?

That's a song.

It *is* a song.

Incorrect.

Keep going.

'A time to tear down a time to build
a time to weep—'

Who are the Byrds?

Incorrect.

There is no *Book of Birds*.

It's a singing group.

'A time to be born
A time to die—'

They stole the lyrics, these Byrds.

From what book?

Anyone?

*what is ecclesiastes*

Correct.

We stare at Jesus, waiting for the next clue, but he says nothing. The room is silent. No one moves. It feels like the game is over. I don't know where to look so I stare at the photo of Vinita and Grace until Jesus starts singing "Turn! Turn! Turn!" as he signs the lyrics. His voice is not good, it's off-key, weak, at times barely audible. Still, his delivery is sincere and heartfelt and I'm so moved I have to leave the room.

# 30

Having him move into her guest room felt exactly like the time she briefly had a puppy that kept her occupied and distracted for weeks. But once the deaf boy was settled in and didn't need her anymore to show him where this was or how to use that, the deaf girl was hit hard with the realization she was alone for the first time in her life; a blow far worse than when she realized, months ago, she had failed at marriage. She had released that failure with a sigh and a shrug as though it were just another one of her failed attempts at a new recipe.

One morning, alone with her coffee, she tried to remember the last time she was single but couldn't. There had always been someone attached to her. Whenever she became unhappy with a boyfriend, certain it was over, she wouldn't break it off until she had another one lined up, covertly test driven and ready to go.

And now she was alone and not alone.

She had assumed correctly that having the deaf boy there, another body in the house, someone to discuss things with, laugh with, eat with, would help her forget everything that was wrong with her life.

Then her father died.

The first day she cried for him. The tears that came after were for her mother. Lourdes put on a brave front as visitors—family, colleagues, students—came and went to the house. But when everyone was gone, her face would collapse as the deaf girl watched. Lourdes would kiss her daughter then go into the bedroom where she would cry openly, loudly, knowing the deaf girl couldn't hear her.

On the day of her father's funeral, while standing in front of the mirror applying lipstick in her mother's bathroom, the sadness that had been coming in waves arrived again with an intensity the deaf girl had never experienced. It started at the top of her head, making her feel flush and faint then slowly moved though her body as if she had swallowed a hot, metallic liquid, a taste she couldn't shake for weeks.

Her first instinct was to start meeting men again, and not for relationships but solely for sex, the language she was most comfortable with, requiring neither signs nor words. The deaf boy seemed the most obvious choice, she thought, his room only a few steps away. Even though she had never thought of him that way, his recent weight loss coupled with his sudden interest in the gym had transformed his body into something she was now attracted to.

One Saturday evening she arrived home and saw steam escaping from the bottom of the bathroom door, spilling into the hallway, reminding her again to have the exhaust fan repaired. Suddenly an image of the deaf boy naked under the shower flashed before her. She removed her clothes, slipped into a robe then lingered in the living room, in the dark, waiting. She watched the bathroom door open. The deaf boy emerged naked, drying his hair with a towel as he headed to his room. She began to undo her robe when another naked young man emerged from the bathroom and followed the deaf boy. She closed her robe, feeling foolish. The next day they talked about it and laughed and that was the end of that.

Then she decided to forget about sex. Whenever a wave of sadness hit her (or an uncomfortable feeling), she would meet up with a girlfriend or two. Or sit in front of the television for hours. Or roam department stores buying things she didn't need. This went on for weeks until one day she decided to take the deaf boy's advice and focus on happy things, but she couldn't find anything that made her happy in her present life so she dug into her past. Every night, hours were spent going through old photos, searching for the ones that made her happy, like a photo of her at four years old wearing headphones with the cord cut off and Mickey Mouse ears attached. For her it was a costume accessory she enjoyed wearing while playing make-believe. Years later, as an adult, her parents confessed the headphones were a desperate attempt to keep the deaf girl from pulling out her hearing aids and losing them.

One night she came across another photo that made her happy, one of her at twelve with a boy named Joaquin Hernandez, a name she instantly remembered. She had first seen him at church where he was an altar boy. She thought he was the handsomest boy she had ever seen with his dark hair and eyes. One Sunday at church, at the end of mass when the parents broke off in groups on the sidewalk, she watched Joaquin as he emerged in street clothes. He bumped into her and she couldn't tell if it was an accident or intentional. He said he was sorry, and when she didn't respond, he apologized again in sign language. This time she responded by running until she was on the side of the church with Joaquin behind her. With no one around, she asked with her hands how did he know she was deaf. He pointed to her hearing aid then explained he had learned sign language to communicate with a cousin who was deaf. He asked her all sorts of questions, with no apparent agenda, no attempt at a kiss or touch like most of the boys she had encountered. For the next three years, until he and his family moved to California, the two of them were inseparable. They never kissed or touched, but she felt something for him though she had no idea what it was.

She was surprised now how many photos of Joaquin she had, some alone, some of the two of them, smiling or laughing, at family picnics, in front of the church, birthday parties. She started to set his photos in a pile to put them in a photo album she planned to look at whenever she needed something to make her happy. In her search for Joaquin photos, she came across a photo from her time at the school for the deaf, the place she was most at home in because she was like everyone else there until the day ended and she had to go back out into the world where she was *special*, her parents always told her. Where most children cried when their parents dropped them off at school, the deaf girl cried when she was picked up, something she confessed now to Jesus and not the Jesus she prayed to but the Jesus that was sitting next to her in Luis' living room.

The first thing she had noticed about this Jesus was the bandages wrapped around the palms of his hands. Ivonne had introduced everyone and she must've said something because Jesus greeted the deaf girl in sign language, which made her smile and her hands signed something back she couldn't remember now because all she was thinking about was how this Jesus looked like Joaquin or how she imagined he would look like now.

She asked Jesus if he was ever an altar boy.

*no*

Or if he had ever lived in California.

*no*

Sometime later, after Cruz had left to take Lourdes home, Ivonne appeared at the kitchen doorway followed by Luis. They began to talk. The deaf girl looked at them, reading their lips and became annoyed when they did something they've been doing all her life, referring to her as *the deaf girl*. This had always bothered her, but she never said anything to anyone except to her mother once, many years ago, who told her daughter that it was simply a nickname meant with love. The deaf girl forced a smile and never mentioned it again.

She asked Jesus how Ivonne had introduced her.

*as my cousin the deaf girl*

She shook her head and turned away when she felt tears begin to surface. Jesus moved in front of her.

*what is your name*

# 31

There were two married professors who had a baby girl.

They named her Ana.

By seven months, the baby had come into her own.

When you called her name, she responded.

When you made funny noises, she laughed.

When a glass shattered, she would startle and cry.

When you sang to her, she smiled and slept.

Then the baby got an infection.

She was sick for a long time.

Then she got better.

But things had changed.

She no longer responded when you called her name.

Or laughed when you made funny noises.

Or startled and cried when something shattered.

Or smiled when you sang to her.

The mother noticed the changes first but said nothing.

When the father noticed, he said something.

She told him it was a temporary thing, sure to go away.

He agreed with her and left it alone.
Until the mother's sister noticed the changes.
The sister made a fuss, a doctor got involved, exams were done.
The infection had damaged the baby's eardrums.
Over time her hearing would continue to deteriorate.
A hearing aid was ordered, the father picked it up.
At home he explained to the mother and her sister how it worked.
Then he proceeded to install the hearing aid on the baby.
But the mother was not convinced it would work.
She knew she would cry when this was confirmed.
She said she'd wait outside and left the room.
The father adjusted the hearing aid.
The mother's sister watched.
Silence.
The father spoke to the baby:
*Ana*
The baby's eyes popped open.
The father made funny noises.
The baby laughed.
The father cried.
The mother's sister left the room to get the mother.
The father sang to the baby, an old Spanish lullaby.
The baby's mouth dropped open.
As if she'd been waiting a long time to hear this song again.

# 32

An accident ahead brings my Granada to a halt on Kingsbridge Road.

"Turn on Webb," Lourdes says. "Then take 195th to Sedgwick."

"If we ever move, I will."

Neither one of us has said a word since we left Luis' apartment. The car radio was playing, but Lourdes asked me to shut it off. Maybe it was too loud. Maybe she didn't like the song. It wasn't until Lourdes pointed to a pizza place she and Javier had eaten at all the time that I thought maybe she's still mourning. Either way the silence now is louder than the music was.

"Vinita worries about you," I say. "We both do."

"I worry about me."

"She feels she's not doing enough for you."

"I've told her there's nothing more she can do."

We're quiet for a long time.

The Granada moves a few inches.

"Lourdes...Why do you think Vinita still goes away?"

"You'll have to ask her that."

"Luis says it's because she doesn't like me anymore."

"Luis? Really? You're going to listen to…?" She shakes her head. "My sister wanted something for a long time, and it slipped away. Now she's restless, that's all. It has nothing to do with you. I wish I had used Luis' bathroom before we left."

An old woman with a plastic grocery bag in each hand hobbles out of breath in front of the Granada. She stops and places a bag on the ground. Wipes sweat away from her face then picks up the bag. She looks at us through the windshield for a moment and moves on.

Lourdes turns on the radio and searches until she hears Celia Cruz singing. After a few seconds, she shuts off the radio and goes on about how she likes Celia's old music better. As she starts listing her favorite Celia songs, I pretend to listen but I'm somewhere else.

\\\\\\

The night before Vinita disappeared, she was standing in the kitchen while I sat at the kitchen table reading the newspaper. She opened the refrigerator and pulled out a red bowl of raspberries she said were whispering, some chant it sounded like, and I couldn't tell if she was joking or not. She sat the bowl on the counter, complaining that it was too red. That it was making the raspberries disappear and she couldn't see them, and if she couldn't see them, how was she going to make her mother's housekeeper's Puerto Rican raspberry rum cake. She opened a cupboard and reached in, searching for something, anything that was not red, she said, and it volunteered, rolling forward into her hand, a blue bowl with white moons and stars that would now take the place of her favorite bowl, a glass thing that had smashed to pieces on the floor yesterday, its contents (white seedless grapes) left where they landed while she went off to take a nap, and when she returned an hour later, I watched her look at the mess with confusion like she had never seen it before. Like intruders, seedless-grape-hating intruders, dogs maybe, had snuck in and made a mess in her kitchen and *how dare these goddamn dogs*, she said. Out of a drawer she retrieved a black marker and wrote on the kitchen wall in big letters *No Dogs or Puerto Ricans Allowed.* Then she threw a handful of raspberries against the letters and they slid down the wall real slow like bloody snails. I was standing next to her, yet Vinita called out my name like I was in the other room. I said her name and she looked at me like I had just entered the room. Kissed me like she hadn't seen me in days then went to bed. The next day she was gone.

\\\\\\

Traffic begins to move again. I turn on Webb Avenue. Lourdes asks what size I am.

"In what?"

"Shirts, pants, shoes."

I'm thinking she's going to ask if I want Javier's belongings. I don't, but I don't want to hurt her feelings so I make up sizes smaller than I think Javier was.

"None of it will fit. I'll donate it. Boy, this whole neighborhood has changed so much.

Sometimes I don't even know where I am. Sometimes I think I've been here too long."

"I think that all the time."

"I wish I was one of those people who could just pick up and go, you know, sell everything and go somewhere else, somewhere different. That's another reason, I think, that Vinita goes away. She walks around here and all she sees is the place she has always struggled in, where the winters are too cold, the summers too hot, where she failed as a mother—"

"She didn't fail."

"We both failed. It's no secret."

"Lourdes..."

She looks at me, waiting for a response, perhaps an argument that proves her wrong.

When I offer her nothing but a dumb look on my face, I'm sure, and an open mouth, Lourdes turns on the radio. After a long weather update, she shuts it off.

"There's nothing easy about it," she says. "Being a mother. I never understood how it comes so naturally for some women while others, like Vinita and I, struggled. Especially if you can't stay focused on your child's needs because you have other things you'd rather be doing, and when you do them, you feel bad or selfish or nothing at all. Can you believe the sun's down yet it's still as hot as ever?"

"Global warming."

"Oh no, you sound like Luis now. Something's going on up there."

Up ahead colored lights are flashing on top of police cars stopped at the intersection.

Lourdes opens the glovebox, digs through it. She pulls out a paper, a receipt probably, for something done to the Granada. She closes the glovebox, fans herself with the paper and says, "There are a lot of us who have no business doing it."

"Doing what?"

"This mother thing. You know, there should be a test you have to pass before you're allowed to be a mother. Like getting a driver's license. You're not allowed to drive until you pass an exam that lets them know you're not going to crash and hurt someone. Didn't that used to be an Indian restaurant?"

I follow Lourdes' gaze out her window. "Taj Mahal. It closed a while ago."

"Just what we need. Another pizza place." She sighs. "And you know what made it harder for me?"

"Hmm?"

"I didn't know how I was doing as a mother until it was too late."

"Those police cars are not going anywhere."

"Not anytime soon—with my students it's a different story. They take my class and I know by the end of the course, by the end of fifteen weeks or so, if I succeeded or not by their grade, but as a mother you have to wait eighteen years, or longer, to see if you succeeded—make a left at this corner—and if you didn't, if you failed, if your child is not doing as well as you hoped because you didn't give them the right tools to, I don't know, hold down jobs, make marriages work, well you can't redo it like taking a class over—oh no, they closed Antonio's."

"About a month ago."

"Why? They were the best bakery in the area."

"They're opening a Dunkin' Donuts."

"What a shame. They had the best croissants. Too buttery for Javier, but I loved them." Lourdes shakes her head. "So what about you?"

"What about me?"

"Have you ever thought of getting out of here."

"Vinita and I have talked about a vacation."

"I meant for good. Move somewhere warm, sunny. I'd hate to see you guys leave, but it'd be good for the two of you. Give you a reason to retire, I mean, you should've retired years ago. Sell the business, the building too, all of it and...just go."

"Vinita said once she'd never move back to Puerto Rico. And California is too expensive."

"There are other places."

Lourdes turns on the radio. She scans the channels until she lands on one of my favorite stations that plays music from the seventies. Roberta Flack is singing "Killing Me Softly." Lourdes mumbles something I can barely hear. Something about Javier and this song. She sings along with Roberta then falls into a whisper that sounds like she's talking to herself. Or Javier.

\\\\\\

Earlier this morning Luis and I stopped at Lourdes and Javier's house. In the past we sometimes found Vinita there rummaging through their garbage. "Lourdes throws things out because she gets tired of them," Vinita said once, "not because they're broken." There was no sign of Vinita there this morning so Luis and I moved on. Then he made a joke I was trying to remember now to share with Lourdes as I pull up in front of her house. An old school desk sits by the curb.

"How did that get there?" Lourdes says.

The front door opens. Vinita steps out onto the porch, dragging another school desk.

Lourdes steps out of the car. "What is she doing?"

I honk the horn. Vinita looks at me then at Lourdes as her sister climbs up the porch steps. They talk. They pick up the desk and carry it to the curb. They go inside then come out with another desk and place it next to the others. I'm thinking I should help them. Then I'm thinking I shouldn't. Don't intrude on their moment. They talk some more. Vinita goes inside and returns with her blue suitcase. There's a hug, a kiss on the cheek. Lourdes waves at me, I wave back. She goes inside.

Vinita crosses the street. I lean over and push open the passenger door. She walks to the rear of the Granada. I step out of the car. By the time I'm halfway towards her, Vinita has placed the suitcase in the trunk and closed it. I get back in the car. She climbs in and sits next to me. A long silence. I want to say something but don't know what to say and this is why, I'm sure, she doesn't like me. Because I don't say anything worthwhile anymore. Because I don't like to go out anymore. Because I stopped making her dresses a long time ago. And maybe I should surprise her and make her something, a summer dress or two. This is what I'm thinking about, summer dresses, when I feel, in the dark of the car, the gentle touch of Vinita's hand on mine that tells me Luis is wrong, that she still likes me. I hope.

# 33

I t was getting dark in the kitchen, yet no one turned on the light. Luis stood in the shadows looking into the living room. On the sofa, with their hands moving in the air, Jesus and the deaf girl sat. Behind Luis, Ivonne was removing knives from a kitchen drawer and throwing them in a bottom cabinet. Luis turned around and looked at her with confusion. He turned on the light and asked what she was doing.

"You have too many knives."

"You can never have too many knives."

"Why do you need so many knives?"

"Why not?"

"Someone can cut themselves reaching in here with all these knives."

"If they cut themselves, I have bandages they can wrap their hands in like your Jesus friend. What happened to him?"

"He fell on glass in a parking lot at a rest stop off of the 80."

"And he landed next to a chihuahua mix—no really. What happened?"

Ivonne gave him a look.

"What? It was too specific. C'mon, I'm big boy, tell me."

"When did you tell me you became a dish collector."

"What?"

"You have dishes in almost every cabinet. Dishes where food should be. You have enough dishes to serve fifty people yet nothing to put on them except stale fucking crackers—"

"I eat out a lot."

"So you don't shop."

"Or cook anymore."

"You don't know how to cook."

"Neither do you."

"But I always have food in my house."

"And someone to cook it for you."

Luis opened a cabinet door then another one.

"Did you get my birthday card?"

"Yes, thanks for the cash—I didn't realize I had so many dishes. Ginger must've been buying them."

"Where is she?"

"Gone."

"Gone to work, gone shopping—?"

"I threw her out a few weeks ago."

"Well good for you."

"Or I came home one day and she had moved out."

"Which is it?"

"I'm not sure."

"You're not sure?"

"I'm not sure."

"You're not sure?"

"Is that it? We're going stand here and repeat each other?"

"Did you throw her out or did she move out?"

"I can't remember how it ended this time."

"So she's not coming back?"

"She's not *welcome* back but that's never stopped her before from *coming* back."

"Why do you even let her in?"

"Because it was getting too expensive to keep changing the lock."

"Where's my purse?"

"Behind you."

Ivonne turned around and reached for her purse on the kitchen counter. She pulled out a pill bottle, read the label then threw it back in the purse. She did that a few times as Luis grabbed a bottle of water from the refrigerator and sat it next to her purse. From the fourth bottle a pill was tapped into her hand, tossed into her mouth and swallowed with water.

"What's that pill for?"

"Anxiety."

"You and Mami and your pills."

"Mami doesn't take pills."

"She takes pills all the time."

"Not for anything serious."

"It must be something serious because she's taken them all my life."

"You don't know anything."

"I know she took a lot of pills."

"Mostly diet pills or vitamins."

Ivonne opened a top cabinet door and found a can of corn. She picked it up and read the label.

"Diet pills?" Luis said.

"Filled with so much caffeine that she can't sleep at night so she takes a pill to help her sleep. She's been doing that forever. Where have you been?"

"I thought they were something serious—hey, did you know Olivia has a cat?"

"She hates cats."

"Well she got one. This nasty thing she thought was a boy then recently found out it was a girl. Named it Cat."

"That's what the writer came up with? Cat?"

"It's short for Catherine."

Ivonne opened the refrigerator. "Catherine. That's not a cat name—my god, I'm starving."

Luis opened a drawer, pulled out take-out menus and threw them on the counter. Ivonne picked up the menus and moved to the kitchen table with her purse and sat down.

"Can I tell you a secret?" Ivonne said, her eyes scanning a menu.

"Don't. I can't keep secrets."

"Sit down."

Luis sat.

"A few months ago, Olivia called me out of the blue. Said she needed some family stuff for her book."

"That's not a secret. She asked everyone. Even Papi."

"Did you send her anything?"

Luis nodded. "Stuff about Ginger and I, but she said 'I know these stories, tell me one I don't know.'"

"She said the same thing to me. 'Mami told me these stories,' she said, 'how about the farm, tell me something about the farm I don't know.' So, bored out of my fucking mind, I sat down one day and wrote until I got sick of writing then sent her what I had and she reads it and sends me notes, stupid fucking notes, stuff like 'You didn't use quotation marks with dialogue. Was that intentional or were you being lazy?' Then she goes off about my commas, didn't like where I placed them and what's wrong with this family, she said, why is everyone so afraid of using a fucking semi-colon and I told her I hate semi-colons."

"I've always hated semi-colons. They're insulting to the reader."

"Exactly. It's like you're saying this thing I just said refers to the thing I said a second ago—"

"But since you're too stupid to put two and two together, I'm going to put this little weird symbol right here so you know they're connected, you fucking moron."

"That's pretty much what I told Olivia and she hung up on me—how's this Italian place?"

"Awful."

"So why do you keep their menu?"

Luis took the menu from her, tore it in half and said, "So the last story I emailed Olivia was about that time when I was a loan officer—"

"You hated that job. I think that's the last time you worked a nine-to-five."

"It was a miserable time—anyway Olivia reads my piece and calls me and starts lecturing me about paragraphs, that I didn't break up my story into a bunch of paragraphs, that when you write one long paragraph, like I did, that it fucks up the reader because the reader needs that little indent at each paragraph, that little white space that gives the reader a visual break, she said, and I didn't know what the fuck she was talking about. Finally I said, 'If the reader needs a break, let him go take a fucking nap' and then she rambles on like she knows what she's talking about because she had a book on the bestseller list—"

"Oh *please*. The only reason she got where she got was because she can sit for long periods of time, always has. Everyone in this family, at one time or another, wanted to be a writer, even Papi, until we actually had to sit down and write. Olivia's done well because she can sit still long enough to finish what she starts because she's got nowhere to go, nowhere to be—well now she does, now she 'teaches' and you know that's not going anywhere because she doesn't know how to be around people, doesn't even know what to do with her hands—and what is she planning to do with these stories we sent her, I mean, she can't use them, she can't pass them off as her own."

"No, they're just...what did she call it...'*Ispirazione*,' which I think is Spanish for I've run out of fucking stories so I'm using yours—"

"That's not Spanish! It's Italian. It means inspiration. Why can't she just say inspiration."

"Since when does she speak Italian?"

"We took Italian in college."

Ivonne looked over a menu, tossed it aside and picked up another one. "It was a language requirement. Spanish was too easy, French too hard...*Ispirazione*. Ugh. All my stories did were inspire her to take a shit, the way she carried on—but you know...my last couple of days have been—I think I'll write about my last couple of days and send it to her and see if that'll shut her up. This restaurant looks good."

"It used to be, but last time everything tasted like it had been sitting under a heat lamp for days."

Ivonne tore the menu in half then picked up another one.

"I think I want Chinese," she said.

"I'm sick of Chinese."

"I haven't had it in three years. They didn't do Chinese near the farm."

"Are you leaving Ben or is this just a temporary thing?"

"I'm calling my lawyer tomorrow. How long has Mami been gone?"

"A week or something like that."

"Do you still run around showing her picture to everyone?"

"Of course."

"You know Mami doesn't really go anywhere anymore, right? I mean she's not hopping on planes to California like she used to."

"Where does she go?"

"If she's just bored, she takes a train to some town in Connecticut and stays with an old Hollywood friend and they sit around and talk about the old days. But if Mami has gained weight, then she takes a train to Queens and stays with another old Hollywood friend whose husband owns a gym there and she eats like bird and comes back all trim again."

"Why hasn't anyone ever told me this?"

"I'm the only one who knows. Besides Mami only told me that a couple of years ago. In case of emergency, she said, like someone died. Do you have a pen?"

Luis moved a stack of mail and papers on top of the table. He found a pen and handed it to Ivonne.

"All this time I thought she was still doing her Hollywood stuff," Luis said.

Ivonne began to circle food items on a Chinese menu.

"She was when we were young," Ivonne said. "But I never believed any of that, her stories about a screen test, some contract that fell through, all that nonsense she used to go on about, without an ounce of evidence. I asked her once if she kept the letter from the studio or *anything* that stated something about an offer of a contract and she said there was no letter, that the studio called her."

"Well she had that old piece of paper with her measurements. From that woman at the studio. She carried that around for years."

"In handwriting that looked exactly like Mami's."

"I believe her."

"I did too until I was about fourteen or fifteen and I noticed whenever she came back from California she never looked exhausted like someone who was out there 'pounding the pavement' as she always called it, no, she always returned rested and tan like she had spent her time out there on the beach, complaining that she was told she was too old even though she was only thirty-something. Then there were those stories about those bit parts in movies she had that for some reason or another ended up on the 'cutting room floor.' My god. Mami and her stories. Believe me, the closest she ever got to the movies was that picture you got in there of her with Grace Kelly on some movie studio Papi worked at for like fifteen minutes—how are their wontons?"

"You can't make a bad wonton."

Ivonne made a few more circles on the menu.

"Okay, I think I ordered enough for all of us. Call this in. I'll pay for it...It's awfully quiet in there."

Ivonne got up from the table. She went and stood at the kitchen doorway and looked into the living room. Jesus and the deaf girl were signing to each other.

"By the way, Aunt Lourdes said Olivia is dating some theatre professor at the university," Luis said. "And I'm only telling you so you know I know things, that I'm not always kept in the dark."

"I'm surprised she's still teaching."

"Aunt Lourdes doesn't think it'll last. She said Olivia wants to write plays now—you know I can't remember the last time the three us of were together. I wish Olivia were here."

"She's here, standing right behind us."

"What?"

Jesus laughed loudly as the deaf girl covered her mouth trying not to laugh.

"Years ago," Ivonne said, "me, Oliva and Mami got together for dinner and she and Mami argued about something. I forget what it was, but it got *really* tense and ugly. Then a year later Olivia's first book comes out and our restaurant scene was in the book."

"I remember that."

"Except Olivia wrote herself out of the scene. It was just me and Mami in the restaurant having this nasty argument, but we're not women anymore, we're men, a father and son. I'm telling you, Olivia is here right now and all this shit we're talking about will be in her next book except she'll write herself out of it and make me look like a bitch."

"You are a bitch sometimes."

"I *know*, but no one else needs to know that, no one needs to read about me in a book and I told Olivia this once and she said, 'It's best to write about what you know' and I said 'Why don't you write about what you don't know. Go make shit up and leave us out of it.' Boy look at them sign."

Jesus and the deaf girl were signing rapidly.

"Can you make out what they're saying?" Luis said.

"If they slowed their hands down..."

The signing stopped.

The deaf girl stared at Ivonne in the doorway, Luis behind her.

"Okay," Ivonne said, "now she's making a face like we farted or something...Here she comes."

The deaf girl was breathing heavily. Then, with her deaf voice, the one she rarely used, she yelled, "Stop calling me the deaf girl!"

Ivonne and Luis froze.

"My name is Ana."

She repeated herself with her hands.

*my name is ana*

*my name is ana*

*my name is ana*

*my name is ana*

*my name is ana*

*my name is ana*

*my name is ana*

And out the front door she went.

The phone rang.

Jesus looked at them and said, "The merciful man doeth good to his own soul: but he that is cruel troubleth his own flesh."

Then he was gone.

Ivonne and Luis stood there with their mouths open. Luis said, "What the fuck was that?"

"Answer the phone!"

"Hello?!"

A voice on the phone said *Happy Birthday* and Luis said, "Where are you, Mami?"

"Home," Vinita said. "My god, Luis, forty years. How awful."

"Thanks, Mami—"

"No, no, no, not your age. It's awful that forty years have come and gone. Your father said Ivonne is in town. Is she still there?"

Luis looked at Ivonne and said, "Is Ivonne still here?"

Ivonne closed her eyes tight and shook her head.

"Luis, tell your sister to get on the phone."

Luis took Ivonne's hand, placed the telephone in it and went into the bathroom. Ivonne took a deep breath and placed the telephone to her ear.

"*Bendicion*, Mami."

"*Dios te bendiga.* Olivia is on her way over so grab your brother and get over here."

"Did you cook?"

"Of course not. I bought a birthday cake for Luis so we can sing to him and give him a proper birthday."

Ivonne was standing in front of the photo of Vinita and Grace Kelly.

"I heard my only grandchild is in Puerto Rico. And you left Ben."

"It's just a separation."

"You said that last time or the time before, then you dragged it out for a year or so. Don't do that to Ben. I actually like him. And please, do yourself a favor, stop getting married."

"I'm just trying to get it right. It's your fault I can't get it right."

"Of course it's my fault. I know that."

Ivonne stared at the photo and said, "Remember a while back you asked me if I had that photo of you and Grace Kelly?"

"Luis has it."

"You knew?"

"Your father just told me. I didn't understand why he didn't bring it with him. So bring it with you."

In the bathroom the toilet flushed.

Ivonne removed the photo from the wall and went into the kitchen with it.

"How old were you in this photo?"

"Same age as Grace. Twenty-three, I think. Do me a favor. Don't let me eat any cake because I lost weight and your father said I look terrific."

Ivonne looked down at her large belly and sighed.

"You know, Ivonne, I can't remember the last time I saw all my children together..."

Three years ago, Ivonne thought. The day before she left for the farm, at some restaurant, and she cried all the way home.

"I don't remember either," Ivonne said. "Luis and I are eating Chinese first, then we'll be over."

"Whatever is left over, bring it with you. I have nothing in the refrigerator."

# 34

Not thinking about the snow was what Vinita wanted to do, was about to do when the photos on the walls suddenly seemed off to her, as if they were all crooked even though they were as level as could be. While Cruz napped in the next room, she interchanged photos, moving them from one nail to another until she was satisfied with all but one photo.

She roamed the apartment now with the photo of her and Grace Kelly, holding it against one wall then another. She felt it should be displayed by itself so it wouldn't get lost among the others, and if one of her children decided to walk off with it again, she'd notice right away.

Luis wasn't even apologetic last summer as he stood in his parents' kitchen and watched Ivonne pull the photo out of her bag and hand it to their mother. Vinita was pleased to have the photo back in her possession though she couldn't help but wonder how her two youngest turned out to be such expert photo thieves. After singing "Happy Birthday" to Luis, Olivia cut into the cake while Cruz pulled out the candles, the knife just missing his fingers. Alcohol was consumed. The mood lightened. Laughter occurred and every other sentence began with *Remember the time when...* As everyone carried on, Vinita stared at the photo, at herself and Grace Kelly, only speaking when a memory that was all wrong or vague was brought up, putting the photo aside to offer dates and details to set the past straight. Her children complained about the heat and humidity and *can we close the windows* and *turn on the air conditioner*, a request that was ignored. And when they began to argue about semi-colons while Cruz dug into another piece of cake, Vinita picked up the photo and left the room.

The snow was coming down heavy now. Vinita looked out the window, at the street, the people, the corner bodega where they were putting out garbage bags and empty boxes. She shook her head at the snow, a hammer in one hand, a nail in the other. She had made so much noise digging through the toolbox in search of what she needed to hang up the photo that she had woken Cruz from his nap.

"Want me to hang that up for you?" he said with a yawn.

"Go back to bed." And he did.

She stood in front of an empty foyer wall and tapped on the nail lightly so as not to disturb Cruz. She hung the photo up and noticed right away it was not flush with the wall. She pushed on the photo then ran a finger around the frame. There was still a gap between the frame and the wall. The nail wasn't hammered deep enough, she thought. She removed the photo and looked at the nail. If she hammered it again, she was sure the nail head would be flush with the wall and that would do her no good. She stepped back and looked at the nail while hugging the front of the photo to her chest. Her hands were crossed against the back of the frame while two fingers tapped against it. Then she felt a slight lump on the back of the frame. She turned it around and ran her fingers along the back of it. It was definitely protruding, probably always was, she thought, but she hadn't noticed while it was surrounded by other frames. She pushed on the lump to flatten it and that worked until the lump popped back up.

The frame lay face down on the kitchen table, its back set off to the side. Inside the frame lay folded pages of old newspaper she had placed there many years ago. She began to remove pages, each one more faded than the previous one. She unfolded one page and examined it closely until she found a date so faded that all she could make out was the year, 1959. She amused herself looking at old advertisements, paying no attention to the news of the day. She set the page aside and picked up another one with a photo of Grace Kelly holding her Oscar for *The Country Girl*, then she was looking at another page filled with movie ads. Next she found a page torn out of a notebook, folded multiple times into a small square; the culprit of the lump in the frame, she was sure of it. She unfolded the page and found her handwriting on it. Each line written in blue or black pen or a pencil that reminded her they were written on different days throughout the year, 1954, written at the top of the page:

*Left Hollywood*
*Back in the Bronx with a baby*
*Cried this afternoon*
*Grace got an Oscar nomination (Mogambo)*
*Snowed all day*
*Changed a lot of diapers again*
*Saw Grace in Dial M for Murder tonight (8/10)*
*Mother's Day, gaining weight*
*Olivia cried all last night, no one slept*
*Saw Grace in Rear Window (I recognized the dress from that day, 10/10)*
*It was so hot today*
*All morning at the laundromat, fun*
*Saw Grace in The Country Girl (no pretty dresses or makeup, raw, 9/10)*
*Cried most of the day*
*Saw Grace in Green Fire (busy girl, does she ever sleep, 3/10)*
*Christmas, gaining more weight*
*More snow*
*Pregnant again*
*New Year's Eve, cried all day*

Vinita read the paper again then put it aside and picked up the last page of newspaper. Another faded date except for the year. 1956. A side-by-side photo of Grace Kelly and Prince Rainier of Monaco.

\\\\\\

*Oscar winner Grace Kelly, 26, one of the highest paid actresses in Holly-wood, announced today she is giving up her career to marry the Prince of Monaco.*

Vinita read the article at the kitchen table with her mouth open while Ivonne, eleven months, sat in a highchair chewing on baby food as Olivia, almost three, stood next to her mother tugging on her house dress. Vinita gave Ivonne another mouthful of baby food and picked up Olivia and sat her at the table in front of a half-eaten bowl of cereal. She read the article again, shaking her head the whole time, baffled that Grace—who was at the top of her game—was giving it all up to become a wife.

Three months after Grace's royal wedding, Vinita and Cruz wait-ed in line one evening at Loew's Paradise Theatre to see Grace—now Princess Grace—with Bing Crosby and Frank Sinatra in *High Society*, her final film. Cruz had his arm around Vinita's waist as they waited to buy tickets. She bit her lip as he nibbled on her ear, kissed her neck. Tickets were purchased.

They made their way through a pair of bronze doors into an inner lobby, and another set of bronze doors that led into the main lobby. Vinita and Cruz, like always, stopped to take it all in, the ceiling with its murals of *Sound, Story and Film*; the marble fountain with a statue of a child on a dolphin, nearby another marble statue of *Winged Victory*; a painting of *Marie Antoinette as Patron of the Arts* over a grand staircase. Then they were looking for seats in the auditorium designed to resemble a sixteenth-century Italian Baroque garden in the eve-ning with twinkling lights above that looked like stars, surrounded by clouds, always making them feel as if they had left the Bronx. They took their seats. The movie began. A musical comedy. Grace looked stunning in one gorgeous dress after another while being pursued by two leading men old enough to be her father. While Cruz and the au-dience laughed, Vinita sat there as if it were a funeral, the death of a career. On their way home, the movie was barely mentioned. Perhaps it was the trivialness of the story that made it so easy for them to forget the whole thing as soon as they had stepped out of the theatre. Yet, as Cruz kissed her on and off, Vinita was overwhelmed with a sadness that lingered for days.

The next day Vinita tiptoed around their apartment doing housework as quietly as she could so as not to disturb her sleeping daughters. She moved slowly in their cramped two-bedroom railroad where one room led into another. She wondered, again, if she had made the right decision a few years ago when the coffee plantation was doing so well that her mother—in a joyous and generous mood—decided she didn't want her daughters to have to wait to inherit her money so she gave them both a huge financial gift. Lourdes used the money as a down payment on a house and Cruz wanted to do the same. But Vinita didn't want a house, remembering her mother, then the housekeeper, working day and night to maintain it, something Vinita had no interest in doing. Instead she had Cruz use the money to buy into the dress factory he worked at, become a co-owner, not just of the business but of the factory building it operated out of. It was the right decision, she thought now as she put away dishes in slow motion to avoid making any noise, exhaustion running through her body from maintaining such a small apartment. They lived modestly but never had to worry about money and she was grateful for that.

She heard a train arriving on the elevated track in the front of the apartment where the living room was located. She heard the windows shaking and braced herself to hear one or both of her daughters cry out for her.

Silence.

Then the sound of the train leaving the station.

Vinita stood in the doorway of her daughters' bedroom. She watched them sleep. She wept quietly for some time then composed herself. Olivia rolled over and continued sleeping. Outside the window, snow began to fall again. Vinita went to the closet and quietly searched inside until she found a small hat box. She took it to the living room, placed the box on the floor and kneeled in front of it. Her hands dug through the box. Headshots of herself. The key to the Hollywood apartment she had once lived in. The photo of her and Grace in a large envelope. Love letters from Cruz. She kept digging in the box until she found what she was looking for: a small piece of paper with her measurements written down years ago.

That night Vinita began to eat like a bird again. Weeks went by and when she didn't trim up as quickly as she wanted, Vinita hired a babysitter without telling Cruz. She instructed the woman to arrive at the apartment after Cruz left for work and depart before he returned. For weeks she used her free time to walk and jog and run up and down any stairs she could find, and when that didn't work fast enough for her, the diet pills began. They made her jittery, giving her more energy than she needed. But they worked.

One morning Vinita read in the paper that Grace Kelly had her first baby, a girl. She thought about the first time she held Olivia when she was born and Vinita was happy for Grace. She stared at the photo in the newspaper of Princess Grace with her baby girl. Years from now, after Grace had become the mother of three, Vinita would watch her be interviewed on television by Barbara Walters who asked a series of benign questions that Grace struggled to answer as if they were complex math problems. The final question was the easiest. *Are you happy?* Vinita expected Grace to say *yes* quickly, without hesitation. Instead, Princess Grace hesitated then said, "I've had plenty of happy moments in my life, yes. I don't think happiness—being happy—is a perpetual state that anyone can be in, no, life isn't that way but, uh…I suppose I have a certain piece of mind, yes…and uh…my children give me a great deal of happiness…and my life here has given me…many satisfactions…" Vinita studied the perplexed look on Barbara Walters' face then turned off the television.

She carefully tore the photo of Grace and her baby girl out of the newspaper. Later that afternoon, while Olivia and Ivonne played with the babysitter in the living room, Vinita stood in a department store with her waist smaller than it had been in years. At the counter she paid for a suitcase that was small, light, sturdy. And blue.

\\\\\\

Vinita put a few of the old newspaper pages back into the frame while leaving the rest on the table. The frame was reassembled. A hand was placed on it. The lump was gone. Cruz entered the kitchen half asleep, talking about ordering a pizza. She asked him to order her a salad. In the foyer Vinita hung the photo on the nail. She ran a finger along the sides of the frame, pleased that it was flush with the wall. She stared at herself and Grace until she heard Cruz's voice ordering dinner. She walked out of the foyer and into the living room. She stood by the window watching the snow coming down, unaware of Cruz in the kitchen reviewing the old newspaper pages on the table, her life in 1954 reduced to a list.

Vinita was startled for a second when she felt Cruz's hand on her shoulder.

"Let's get out of here," he said.

"I thought we're eating in."

"Out of the Bronx."

"Where would we go?"

"Somewhere else...somewhere warm."

She grabbed his hand off her shoulder and kissed it. They stood by the window for a long time, looking down at the street, at a man sprinkling salt on the sidewalk, children throwing snowballs at each other, cars covered in snow moving at a glacier's pace.

# 35

na has a new friend named Joseph.
He used to go by the name Jesus.
He lives with her and her deaf friend Lucas.
He sleeps on the sofa.
In the summer, the front door is left open.
The foyer light over *Guernica* is always on.
It spills onto the porch.
This is where they sit every night.
Where they drink wine and tell stories.
As their hands move like ninjas.
Tonight Ana signs about *Guernica*.
How Picasso painted it in Paris.
After the bombing of Guernica in Spain.
It lives in Madrid now, some museum.
*The painting is about marriage.*
*Marriage?*
*That's what my grandmother Dolores said.*
The men disagree, it's about war.

*Some marriages are war.*
They stop signing and stare at *Guernica.*
More wine is poured, a joke is told.
Ana laughs down the porch steps.
Laughs onto the sidewalk.
Joseph and Lucas behind her, laughing.
She stops at the curb.
She wants to sign something.
But doesn't.
Too many neighbors out.
She looks back at the house.
Sees *Guernica* framed in the doorway.
Sees her grandmother on the porch.
Dolores smiles and signs.
Ana runs out into the street.
She waves at her neighbors.
Cars are stopping, honking.
Maybe it was all the excitement.
Or the wine.
Or the summer heat.
But she does it, right there.
In front of the neighbors.
She signs.
About everything.
Signs until she has nothing left to say.

# 36

(*SCENE:*

*Cruz and Vinita's Apartment. Bronx, NY.*

*In the darkness, voices are heard. A SLIDE appears on the rear wall of the stage:*

**1998**

*The slide disappears as LIGHTS come up on VINITA and OLIVIA standing in the LIVING ROOM surrounded by moving boxes. Olivia is roaming the room, picking up and examining knickknacks while Vinita throws things in boxes or a trash can in the middle of the room.*)

VINITA

...You're on the wrong side.

OLIVIA

Of what?

VINITA

Of the room.  Everything on *this* side I'm taking, everything on *that* side is up for grabs.

OLIVIA

I can't believe you're taking all that.

VINITA

These things have been with me a long time.

OLIVIA

I don't understand you.  All these years you were always fine going away with everything you needed in a little blue suitcase and now you need all this stuff—why are you even taking any of this?

VINITA

Because the stuff on this side is tied to a memory, a good one, and on days that I'm feeling off, I can pick up something on this side and maybe not feel so off. Now get back on that side.

*(Vinita resumes putting things in boxes while Olivia wanders the room.)*

VINITA

How's the theatre professor?

OLIVIA

I have no idea.

VINITA

Are you two over already?

OLIVIA

Yes, and let's talk about something else.

VINITA

How's your play coming along?

OLIVIA

Oh my god. Can anyone in this family keep their mouth shut?

VINITA

Am I going to see this in it?

OLIVIA

What?

VINITA

*This*.  Us chatting here.

OLIVIA

Of course not.

VINITA

Just don't have me swear.

OLIVIA

Excuse me?

VINITA

In your first book, the mother swears.  I don't swear.  You swear, your brother and sister swear, but I don't.

OLIVIA

Note taken.

VINITA

There's a few things on that shelf Luis didn't take yesterday because he thought you'd want them.

OLIVIA

There's nothing on this shelf I want.  Ask Ivonne.

VINITA

She wants nothing.

OLIVIA

When did she come by?

VINITA

She hasn't.  She's not.  She just said she wants nothing.

OLIVIA

Do you know why she's not talking to me?  She won't respond to my calls or emails.  I thought maybe she's just busy with that house she bought.

VINITA

She's not talking to Luis either.

OLIVIA

Do you know why?

VINITA

Because your grandmother left you and Luis a lot more money than her.

OLIVIA

I didn't know that.  How does she know that?

VINITA

I told her.

OLIVIA

Why would you tell her that?  My god, Mami, you know how she is about money.

VINITA

(As she tapes a box closed.)

It just came out.  Your grandmother didn't come to New York often, but when she did, she would notice how Ivonne always had a new house or husband, always wore expensive jewelry and clothes and she'd take us to fancy restaurants in the city or a Broadway show or both and I told Ivonne this and she said, "I shouldn't be punished for making smart decisions." Like marrying for money is a smart decision.

*(Olivia picks up a small vase and examines it.)*

OLIVIA

I worry about her.  All that money and she's still as miserable as ever.

VINITA

That vase would look nice in your apartment.

OLIVIA

I can't decide if I like it or not.  Is there a story behind it?

VINITA

A story?

OLIVIA

Did it belong to anyone from the old days?  A great-uncle from the island or—

VINITA

Oh god no. I rescued it from your Aunt Lourdes' trash. I was with her when she bought it many years ago at Alexander's on Fordham Road. Remember Alexander's? They used to be everywhere, then they weren't.

OLIVIA

*(Making a face at the vase.)*

I don't like it. Should I toss it?

VINITA

No. When you're done, I'm having the neighbors come over to take what they want.

*(Olivia places the vase back in its place.)*

VINITA

*(After a long pause.)*

So did you decide?

OLIVIA

On what?

VINITA

On what you are going to do with your grandmother's money?

OLIVIA

I'm still getting over her death.  Haven't given any thought to how I'm going to spend her money though it's going quickly.

VINITA

Don't do that again.

OLIVIA

What?

VINITA

Every time you get money—book advances, loans from us, that time you won the lottery—you can't spend it fast enough and you're back to having nothing.  It's like you enjoy struggling.

OLIVIA

I don't enjoy it.

VINITA

You know it's okay to have, to not struggle.

OLIVIA

I need to struggle. Artists are supposed to struggle, everyone knows that, it's a cliché that's been around forever. If you don't struggle, then you're not a real artist, you're a cashier or something.

VINITA

That's nonsense.

OLIVIA

It's the truth.

VINITA

It's nonsense. You're just scared of that other thing.

OLIVIA

What other thing?

VINITA

Success.

OLIVIA

Did Luis tell you that?

VINITA

Probably.  Someone else always has to tell me what's going on with
you.  Your first novel was on the bestseller list, and if your Aunt
Lourdes didn't read the *Times* all the time, none of us would've
known.  You always keep everything to yourself.  You always have.
I hate not knowing what's going on with my children.  And now that
we're moving across the country, I'll never know what's going on with
any of you.

OLIVIA

I still can't believe you guys are moving to Phoenix.  That I won't be
able to see you guys anytime I want.

(*Olivia looks at a small box.*)

VINITA

You never see us.

OLIVIA

But I can if I want to.

(*Reading box.*)

"Kids Drawings." This one is sealed.  Shouldn't it be on that side of
the room?

VINITA

I'm not taking that. Your father packed that years ago. It's been sitting in the back of a closet. It's drawings the three of you made in school. I thought you'd all want them, but Luis wasn't interested and Ivonne, well—

OLIVIA

Are they any good?

VINITA

I don't know. It was your father who collected them. Last time I saw any of them was when he'd hang them on the refrigerator until one of you brought home a new one. I always thought he was throwing them out—anyway I think you should keep them since you're the family historian.

OLIVIA

I'm not the family anything.

VINITA

Yes, you are, the way you write about our past.

OLIVIA

My characters are not this family.

VINITA

Are you hungry?

OLIVIA

No. When are you guys leaving?

VINITA

Tuesday.

(*Olivia examines a candle holder.*)

OLIVIA

Phoenix.

VINITA

It was not my first choice. I mean I don't *not* like it. We went there twice years ago. Scottsdale area mostly. I wanted to move to California, but your father reminded me that our money would last four times longer in Phoenix, that houses with a pool were much, much cheaper in *Phoenix*.

OLIVIA

I was in Phoenix one summer. On a book tour. All I remember was it was very hot. Like someone had set me on fire.

VINITA

But it's dry.

OLIVIA

Heat is heat.

VINITA

But you don't have to shovel it.

OLIVIA

Well it's not like you shovel snow now. The super does that. Papi says you won't even go out when it's snowing anymore.

VINITA

Ugh...You'll have to visit us in the winter.

*(Vinita closes a box with packing tape. Olivia examines a small statue.)*

OLIVIA

*(Holding up the statue.)*

I gave you and Papi this for Christmas years ago. You went on and on about how much you loved it. Shouldn't it be on that side?

VINITA

Olivia, either take stuff or don't.

(Olivia tosses the statue into the trash can.)

VINITA

You know Phoenix is about an eighty-minute flight to Hollywood.

OLIVIA

There's no airport in Hollywood. You fly into L.A. then drive to Hollywood.

VINITA

Don't forget to check those boxes in the corner.

OLIVIA

I've seen enough...How are you feeling?

VINITA

Fine.

OLIVIA

Really?

VINITA

What?

OLIVIA

Grandmother being gone.

VINITA

It hasn't really hit me yet. I've been so busy. The funeral, the flying back and forth to look at houses, packing. I'm sure once your father and I move and settle down, it'll hit me and I'm not looking forward to that day. Will you be able to make it to your Aunt Lourdes'?

OLIVIA

For what?

VINITA

Our farewell party.

OLIVIA

On Saturday. I'll be there.

(Glances at her watch.)

I have to go. I have a class.

VINITA

How's that going?

OLIVIA

Teaching is not for me.  You have to care and I don't care.

VINITA

Think of it as a day job.

OLIVIA

*(After a pause.)*

Mami...

VINITA

Hmm?

OLIVIA

I don't want it to be like that bestseller list thing again.

VINITA

What are you talking about?

OLIVIA

*(After a pause; a whisper.)*

I sold the film rights to my first novel. I've known for a while. Don't know why I haven't told anyone.

VINITA

That's *wonderful...*

> *(Vinita is visually moved. She is trying not to cry. She goes to Olivia and hugs her. They pull apart. For the rest of the scene, Olivia whispers and speaks as if she's embarrassed by it all.)*

OLIVIA

My agent says it could take a year or longer before anything happens, you know, if it'll actually be a movie, but he says there are important people signing on to the project so it shouldn't sit forever in *development hell*, as he called it. They're talking about pairing me up with some big shot screenwriter to adapt my book and he says I can write from here but it, uh...uh...

VINITA

What?

OLIVIA

That it would be better for my career to move to Los Angeles, but I don't know if I could do that.

VINITA

*(A whisper.)*

Of course you can.  It'd be so easy for you.  You have no husband, no children, nothing keeping you here...You're the only one of my children born out there so it makes sense you end up back there.  And your father and I will only be eighty minutes away.  I can come visit you anytime I want and I will...Olivia, go...*Go.*

*(Olivia looks at her watch. She kisses Vinita and exits. Vinita stands there smiling for a while. She goes up to the box marked KIDS DRAWINGS. She stares at it for a few seconds then pulls on the tape and unseals the box. She reaches in and pulls out some drawings. As she views each one, they appear as SLIDES on the rear wall of the stage:*

(*The last drawing vanishes from the rear wall as Vinita places the drawings back in the box. Vinita closes the box as the lights begin to dim. She picks up the box and moves it to the other side of the room.*

*Lights out.*)

# 37

ad inspiration not abandoned Cruz, Vinita's dress would've been finished on July 14, 2000, exactly three days after her death. Everyone urged him not to make a dress, to simply buy one, something classic, not too fancy. *It's a funeral for God's sake, not a cocktail party*, Ivonne reminded Cruz in the middle of their Hitchcock marathon. She was staring at the television, one hand fanning herself, the other clinging to a water bottle. Her lower body was trapped in blue shorts that were two sizes too small, making it difficult for Cruz to distinguish between his daughter and the blue chair she was sitting on. He lay nearby on a chaise lounge covered in paisley chenille, the Jean Harlow Fainting Sofa, Vinita called it, an antique purchased last year in Los Angeles. She loved it in the showroom, then, within days of it being delivered, complained that its soft curves clashed with the stark lines of their modern Arizona home. Cruz suggested they return the chaise to which she said, "I'd rather sell the house and move."

Cruz stretched out on the chaise. He wrapped his right arm behind his head, matting down his hair, grey only a week ago, now black, *so* black that it startled Ivonne and Luis when he picked them up yesterday at Phoenix's Sky Harbor Airport. They stood at the baggage claim, not staring at the bags going by but at their father's hair. *The color is Clairol Natural Black for men*, Cruz explained, *but there is nothing natural about it*, Luis said. He stopped staring at his father's hair while Ivonne kept commenting on it, but her comments went unnoticed because Cruz was too distracted, unsettled, puzzled, once again, by her sudden weight gain. He and Vinita had visited Ivonne—at her request—a year ago in the Bronx, sitting with her while she finalized her divorce from the farmer/dentist. Ivonne was miserable but thin and now look at her, my god, what happened, Cruz had wanted to say when they entered the airport parking lot. But his children wouldn't give him a chance to say anything, hitting him with all sorts of questions he wasn't ready to answer. But once they got inside the Granada, it was as if Ivonne and Luis were children again and Vinita was sitting in the front seat complaining about a headache, instructing everyone to be quiet and they were now, distracted by the view outside their windows.

Cruz pulled out of the airport and drove the Granada onto the freeway. He stared at the Arizona sky that was always blue, yearning for rain or, at the very least, an overcast day. He thought about Vinita, replaying—for the third time that day—their last conversation. They were sitting on dining room chairs they had dragged in front of the glass patio doors that faced the yard. They were talking about their upcoming trip to Los Angeles to stay with Olivia in her condo. Both of them whispering as if the house were filled with sleeping babies. Staring out the patio doors at the pool they had to have but never used because it was either too hot out or neither one of them wanted to get their hair wet. Staring at clay pots and desert plants and lounge chairs and all sorts of southwestern décor that never moved. They looked forward to Thursdays when the stillness was disturbed by their gardener moving back and forth.

"I thought Olivia was in London," Cruz whispered to Vinita that night.

"She might be," Vinita whispered. "We'll use the keys to get in. I'm going to bed."

Vinita stood up and turned to leave then stopped. She reached out and placed a hand on the back of a chair. Cruz asked if she was okay, but she didn't answer, didn't look good either. He helped her sit back down, asked if she had one of her headaches again, if she wanted to go to the hospital. She shook her and said, "Just hold me." He moved his chair in front of hers, leaned in and held her for some time. 0Then she pulled away, smiled and whispered, "Well that passed, whatever it was." She kissed Cruz and headed to the bedroom. He watched as she stopped in the living room in front of a black-framed movie poster, the film version of Olivia's first book. "I like this frame much better," she said. Vinita went to bed and never got up again.

Ivonne stared at the television at a Hitchcock movie. She shifted her body in the blue chair, lifted her blouse and undid the top button of her shorts. The door in the kitchen that led to the garage opened. Luis entered the room carrying a large box.

"What happened to you?" Ivonne said.

"Hmm...?"

"You went to check the gas level in Papi's car. That was twenty minutes ago."

"What's in the box?" Cruz said.

Luis sat the box on the floor and pulled out an old shade from the Santana Bay. He unrolled it revealing El Morro, torn and faded.

Ivonne made a face and looked away.

"Where are the other two, Papi?"

"That's the only one left."

"I've searched online for these for years."

"You won't find those online. An artist in Puerto Rico hand-painted those, gave them to your grandmother and she sent them to us. So we could be reminded of where we came from, her note said. When your mother and I saw them, we made a face and laughed and she dared me to put them up, but they were too big for the windows but that didn't stop me. I had them cut down and—as a joke for an upcoming party—I installed them and left them rolled up, didn't even tell your mother. Later that night our apartment was filled with Puerto Ricans drinking and dancing and I did my big reveal. I stopped the music. I rolled the shades down and the room got quiet and Vinita and the guests didn't laugh, they just stared at the shades, at El Morro and the ocean and the sun and cried like I did and...I never got around to taking them down."

"They were tacky," Ivonne said.

"I'm taking this one," Luis said. "Where's Mami's blue suitcase?"

"Olivia is taking it."

"Oh...Let me go put this in my room. What time do I need to leave?"

Luis placed the shade back in the box.

"The airport's about twenty minutes away," Cruz said.

"Is there enough gas in the car?" Ivonne said.

"I guess."

"Stop for gas."

Luis picked up the box and left the room.

"Hear that, Papi? He called his guest room *my* room. You're never going to get rid of him."

"He can stay as long as he wants."

"He did nothing with all that money Grandmother left him except buy a cell phone and travel Europe to do readings. I go over there to relax and sightsee and my brother goes to talk to dead people. You know he has a website where he promotes himself, sells his services, even has testimonials from clients raving about him."

"I didn't know that."

"He's not cheap either. He must be doing well, because it's been forever since he's called me for money. This is my favorite scene." She stared at the television. "The way Hitchcock does the whole thing with no dialogue, just music."

"I think Luis—"

"Shh..." Ivonne pressed the remote and turned up the volume.

Cruz took a deep breath, held it for a few seconds then exhaled. He picked up his sketch pad off the coffee table and thumbed through it. He examined dress designs for Vinita he was mildly content with a few days ago until Ivonne arrived and insisted the dress be white. He wanted to remind her that Vinita was not a fan of white for dresses unless you were a bride. But to avoid an argument, Cruz agreed with his daughter and that was when his inspiration abandoned him. Suddenly every design looked like a wedding dress gone wrong.

Ivonne dropped her water bottle. Cruz watched as she struggled to get out of the blue chair, moving as if she were wearing something heavy, a space suit or oxygen tanks, her face distorted, groaning as she bent over, sighing when she snatched the bottle off the floor. She placed it on an end table, next to a mosaic wood box with inlays of bone and mother of pearl where Vinita had kept her jewelry since the fifties. Ivonne picked up the jewelry box and started going through it, holding up items, appraising them. "I can't tell which one of these is the cheapest," she said. "It'd be such a waste to bury Mami in something expensive. Something I'm sure she'd want me to have, I mean, Olivia and Aunt Lourdes have never been into jewelry. Neither one even wore earrings to any of my weddings—oh my, I've always loved this." She tried on a ring and admired it.

Cruz looked away. He reached for a black mug filled with coffee. He took a sip then examined the mug, its sides painted with colorful specks, confetti perhaps, and balloons, all floating around the number 70. It was a birthday gift, this mug, from Lourdes, received in the mail a few months ago. Cruz took another sip and returned the mug to the coffee table, turning it, slowly, until the number 70 faced away from him. He was looking at the television, at Thelma Ritter displaying her acerbic wit when Ivonne brought up Vinita's dress again, making a case, as she had been since she arrived, for the purchase of a dress, especially now, with only forty-eight hours left until the funeral. "And we have to have a dress before Olivia gets here," she said, "because you know her, you know what she'll do, she'll say nothing then go off and put this whole goddamn scene in a book and say it's not about us, but it will definitely be about us and people will ask me *was your father that off*, I mean, do you want people to ask if you were this off—?"

"Olivia..."

Cruz was looking past Ivonne. She turned around and saw Olivia standing there with a suitcase. She placed it on the floor and went to Cruz. They hugged for a long time. When Ivonne heard Olivia crying, she turned away.

The crying stopped, the hug ended, and Cruz said, "We thought you were arriving tomorrow."

Olivia pulled out tissues, wiped her eyes and said, "My meetings ended early."

"I thought you were staying at a hotel," Ivonne said.

"I never said I was."

"I just assumed. With you being a Hollywood writer, winning awards and all."

"Nominations are not awards. I've won nothing. Where's my brother?"

"Where is she sleeping, Papi?" Ivonne said.

"There are twin beds in Luis' room," Cruz said. "You guys can switch rooms."

"Hey Olivia..." Luis said, entering the room.

"Hey, little brother."

Luis went right into Olivia's arms and wailed. Cruz turned and looked out the patio doors. Ivonne stared at the television. Then the room got quiet except for the sound of a piano playing coming from the television. Olivia and Luis separated.

"I have to go to the airport," Luis said, "and pick up Aunt Lourdes and Ana—"

"I'd love to go."

"Oh good. It's early, but I'd like to leave now and stop for a slice of pizza."

"You won't find a slice of pizza around here," Cruz said. "This isn't New York. Here they make you buy a whole pie with all sorts of toppings you've never heard of or want."

"We'll find something."

Luis went out to the garage. Olivia took Ivonne aside and whispered, "What's going on with Mami's dress?"

"He hasn't even started it yet."

"Well stay on him."

"He hasn't sewn in years. You know it's going to look like shit."

"He just wants to contribute. It'll be fine."

"If he doesn't come through, I'll just pull something out of Mami's closet."

"And have her be seen in something she's already worn? My god, she'd never stop haunting us. I'll buy her a dress when I'm out."

The Granada's loud horn sounded in the garage, startling them.

"Make sure you have Luis stop for gas," Ivonne said.

"I thought you had gotten rid of this." Olivia touched Ivonne's stomach.

"I did, but it came back, son of a bitch."

"You're just bored. Find something else to do besides count your money."

Ivonne hit Olivia on the arm. "I don't count my—"

"When's the last time you worked?"

Ivonne tilted her head, her mouth dropped open, deeply stumped by the question.

Olivia smiled, hugged Ivonne and whispered in her ear. *I miss you.* Then she was gone.

Ivonne turned to Cruz. He was looking out the patio doors at a lizard posing in front of a terra-cotta pot, its blue skin blending in then disappearing into the pot's pattern, a mosaic of miniature turquoise tiles. Animal and pot were now art framed by the Arizona desert that rose above the brick wall surrounding the yard, the sky mostly clear except for a few clouds above the red rock mountains. Cruz stared at the lizard, his blue buddy, B.B., he called him, frozen now like one of those little toys Ivonne used to terrorize Luis with when they were young.

"Why do you have four bedrooms?" Ivonne said.

Cruz turned away from the patio doors. "Because when my children visit at the same time, I don't want any of you to have to share a room."

"You and Mami were here for two years and this is the first time we're all here together. And guess what? I'm sharing a room."

"I didn't expect your aunt and cousin to be here at the same time."

"Yeah well..." She picked up the water bottle and sipped on it.

"You can have my room. I'll sleep out here."

"I'm fine sharing. I was just wondering why you bought such a big house for two people—" Ivonne coughed and spilled water on her blouse, a lot of it.

She moved past Cruz and swung the sliding patio door open, savagely, as if she were back on a Bronx subway, switching cars, looking for that last empty seat. B.B. ran behind the terra-cotta pot, past a large cactus then disappeared into the desert garden. Ivonne removed her blouse. She picked up a towel folded over the back of a lounge chair, threw it aside and placed her blouse in its place. She stood there in her bra and shorts. "Could it get any goddamn hotter."

"I have neighbors you know," Cruz said.

She waved him off and jumped into the pool.

Cruz closed the patio door. Ivonne got out of the pool and lay in a lounge chair. She pointed past Cruz and yelled something that sounded like *Get to work*. He turned around. On the dining table sat the Singer, model #AJ-242, his first sewing machine, a dinosaur purchased in 1950, recently dragged out of storage after Cruz had given up on a newly purchased Singer, a modern machine as confusing to him as the dashboard of a jet, the damn thing completely uncooperative. He had hit it with a broomstick and put the whole thing in the trash.

Cruz walked up to the dining table and looked at this dinosaur that seemed to scream in protest when he had it picked up and taken it away to be serviced. When Ivonne saw it, she looked at Cruz as if he were insane, but he didn't care. He knew he had to make the dress, a decision he made on the night he had to call his children and tell them their mother was gone, his voice soft, slow, every word a struggle to get out as if he had swallowed glass. Everyone cried on the telephone except Ivonne, silent for so long Cruz thought she had hung up.

"Are you still there?" he said.

"What did she die of?"

"They don't know. They said if I wanted an autopsy done, but I can't have them cut her up."

"There's no need for an autopsy. I visited you guys twice and Mami was always busy decorating the house and I thought what is she going to do when she hangs up that last picture and she finally did and there was nothing else to do. She clearly died of boredom..." Ivonne paused on the telephone and Cruz could hear a pill bottle rattling, water running, a gulp of water taken. "...And you tried to compensate with frequent trips to Los Angeles, both together and apart, with her sometimes going off on her own—openly—with no need for her to sneak off and where was the fun in that."

"I have to go—"

"Mami particularly loved the time Olivia took her to the studio, dragging her through movie sets, recreations of scenes from her book, from our lives, introducing Mami to movie stars and what not—my god, she was in heaven until she returned to Phoenix elated and equally miserable and didn't know why, she told me on the phone, then she began to ramble about baseball and balls and nonsense and suddenly she had nothing to say and we hung up and later that night I was in bed and I thought of Mami and her rambling and it wasn't about baseball and balls at all, it was about her, she was talking about herself when she said the ball was dropped, *she* dropped the ball, and I kept calling her every week and she never had anything to say anymore. It was like she finally accepted, Papi. It had died, her dream, and she was in mourning, completely numbed, as though her mother had died all over again...When's the funeral?"

And Cruz didn't authorize an autopsy.

But not knowing the cause of death ate away at him so much that he did what he didn't want to do. When Luis arrived, he took him aside and asked him how his mother had died.

"Jesus, Papi. All my life you've always given me a hard time about... *that*...and now— No. No, you don't get to know."

"So she came to you?"

"Of course she did. I was her baby boy—"

Luis covered his mouth with a hand, not completely sure if he'd said what he'd said out loud or if he had just thought it. He turned around and left the room. They didn't speak again until later that night when Luis went to get something from the garage and found Cruz sitting in the Granada, his head on the steering wheel, crying. Luis started to go back into the house then stopped. He opened the passenger door and slid into the front seat. Cruz raised his head from the steering wheel, wiped his eyes and looked straight ahead. Luis whispered *Mami* then paused for a few seconds. After he told Cruz what he wanted to hear, after his father wept on his shoulder, Luis went back into the house.

Cruz sketched another dress design now, then another and another, each one ending up in the trash. He sat in front of the dinosaur, staring at it until he heard the patio door open. Ivonne sighed as she entered the cool room wearing her blouse.

"Can you believe this?" she said. "I didn't even use a towel and I'm already dry. It's like standing in a giant dryer out there."

She moved to the kitchen counter and began to unscrew the caps on the salt and pepper shakers. Cruz watched her refill them as she leaned against the counter, her right foot rubbing against the back of her left leg. The phone rang. Ivonne answered it. *The dress is almost ready*, she said, then gave Cruz a look. He looked away and stared at the dinosaur, the thing suddenly reminding him of the first sewing machine he had used at twelve years old when he stepped on his first pedal. That machine belonged to Mrs. Palladio, an old Italian woman with paralyzed legs who lived in his Bronx neighborhood, who gave him five cents every Saturday to press the foot pedal while she made dresses, barking in her shrill Italian, *Vada*, he'd press the pedal, *Arresto*, he'd stop. Her Italian followed him around for years, even when he worked briefly at Paramount and the other seamstresses would stare at him, fascinated by this Puerto Rican who chanted while he sewed, not in Spanish, but Italian, *vada, arresto, vada, arresto.*

Ivonne hung up the phone. "That was the undertaker. He needs the dress by the end of the day."

She returned to the salt and pepper shakers, wiping them down then putting them back in their place, humming an old Spanish song Cruz was trying to recognize. It made him think of Vinita and Cruz said her name, softly, over and over as he looked around the room, feeling lost as if he were in a stranger's house. He looked down at fabric samples sitting on the table, all different colors. He picked up a sample and rubbed it between his fingers then tossed it aside while Ivonne pulled out lemons from the refrigerator. He went to the patio doors and looked out. Cruz placed a hand on the glass, feeling the heat, wishing he could go for a walk, but the desert sun no longer provided relief for his bones, just torture with its unrelenting heat that had kept him inside for the last two days sketching pages and pages of garbage, sketches that now lay nearby crumpled up and gathered in packs like jagged snowballs that refused to melt.

Something fell behind him.

Cruz turned around and saw Ivonne struggling to get a lemon that had rolled under the table, then they were sitting at another table in some restaurant in the Bronx, many years ago, when Ivonne was young and thin and beautiful like her mother who was sitting with them at the table. They were having lunch. Vinita had just asked Ivonne how could she not invite Olivia to her wedding because of some silly argument. Cruz chimed in and scolded Ivonne who replied casually, "Olivia won't be missing anything." Everyone fell silent. Vinita asked if she loved this man and Ivonne said, "Mami, if I waited until I fell in love, I'd never get married. I have to go. I have to look at more dresses, that's right, I still don't have a wedding dress because my father's too busy to make me one." Ivonne stood up in the restaurant and turned to walk away. Vinita grabbed her hand and pulled her back and they looked at each other. Tears filled Ivonne's eyes. She kissed her mother and pulled away as Cruz reached into his jacket, pulled out a folded paper and handed it to Ivonne. She opened the paper and found a sketch of a wedding dress that left her breathless.

With lemon in hand, Ivonne used a dining chair to get herself up off the kitchen floor, completely out of breath. Cruz left the room and wandered the house, moving very slowly as if he were suddenly at the bottom of the ocean, each step getting heavier and heavier. He went from room to room, opening closets, rummaging through drawers, looking for nothing in particular. In the hallway, Cruz stared at old photos until Ivonne handed him a glass of lemonade. She took his hand, led him to the dining table and sat him in front of the dinosaur, then she went off to her room. Cruz stood up and lay on the chaise and stared at the television, at the actors. James Stewart. Grace Kelly. Thelma Ritter. Cruz studied Grace's dress, impressed with its simplicity, trying to recall the year the film was made, the same year he had met Edith Head on the Paramount backlot, who treated the seamstresses like family, including them in everything, even her Hollywood parties that Cruz attended with Vinita who always dressed in something

Cruz had made her, turning heads all night as she walked through Edith's ballroom, her head tilted up, her eyes always mesmerized by the room's centerpiece, an oversized five-tier chandelier ornamented with gold leaves and distressed crystal drops, its lights causing everything it touched to shimmer, every glass, every sequin, every diamond necklace, every satin lapel on every black tuxedo that often gathered in herds and moved through the room like an oil spill in a sea of dresses made of satins, taffetas, chiffons, ice blue being the dominant color that year. They were far from the Bronx and Vinita loved it, this new world painted from her dreams.

Cruz sketched another dress then immediately crumpled it. Again he roamed the house. The large entry foyer. The master bedroom. The former den, now library. A library in name only as reading was never done in this room despite the floor-to-ceiling bookcases, their shelves filled with leather-bound books, all French, all hand-picked by Vinita in some used bookstore in Los Angeles. She had chosen the books, she said, for their multi-colored surfaces that complimented the colors in the drapes that ran along the windows. No one ever touched these foreign books except the housekeeper who dusted them every Saturday. And even if Vinita and Cruz wanted to touch them, to read them, they couldn't, for neither one of them knew a word of French. Cruz looked at the painting over a brown leather sofa. A reproduction of Cézanne's *Still Life With Basket*, the painting's hues echoing the surfaces of the leather-bound books. There was nothing in the library Cruz was attached to. Everything was there because it all matched, and *I love that*, Vinita had said, exhausted, once again, by another house project that went on way too long.

Cruz left the library. Moments later he lay on the tile floor in the living room where it was cooler, in this spot, in this place where Cruz could think, staring at the television, his eyes on Grace Kelly in *Rear Window*, pacing in a courtyard, near a garden, wearing a sleeveless ivory dress embroidered with copper-colored flowers, a dress Cruz had altered, a lifetime ago, so that Grace could climb, without constraint, the fire escape she was now ascending as James Stewart watched in horror.

Cruz pressed his back into the cool tile floor. His head was a few inches from the patio door. He admired the way the sunlight added a golden tint to the salmon walls, creating a whole new color. Cruz turned his head to catch a glimpse of the setting sun and found himself face to face with B.B. The lizard's face was practically pressed against the glass. They stared at each other. Then the blue creature began to turn, in spurts, as if he were playing some child's game. Green light, he turned a bit. Red light, he froze, green, B.B. turned some more, until finally his back was to Cruz, a back that was not blue at all like the front. A back that looked as if the lizard had been caught in a storm of golden rain, the drops now dried on green bands, a rich olive green accented with vanilla specs, then, tying it all together, a black stripe across the neck like the chokers women wore in the fifties.

B.B. turned to the side, froze, then ran off.

In the garage Cruz dug through a bin filled with bolts of fabric of different colors. He explored all shades of blues and greens. Sometime later Cruz was sketching, then he was cutting fabric, then he was feeding it into the mouth of the dinosaur, his foot on the pedal, hesitantly at first, pressing the pedal while pushing the fabric, pressing, then releasing his foot on the pedal, then pressing some more. Overwhelmed, Cruz stopped sewing and Vinita entered the room, young, her hair in a bun, looking stunning in an evening gown Cruz had made her, a strapless teal dress with a slit no one was doing yet, a mink stole in one hand, pearls in the other.

"We're going to be late," Vinita said.

She handed the pearls to Cruz and turned around. He placed them around her neck, followed up with a kiss on her bare shoulders. "Beautiful. Look at you. Like you've never even had a baby."

"Thank you, but J.J. would disagree."

"When am I going to meet this J.J.?"

"Soon. Will Gary Cooper be there tonight?"

"Not sure. But Brando is."

"You didn't tell me he was filming at Paramount."

"He's not, he's shooting at Columbia with Kazan. I overheard Edith say he was going to be there."

"Promise me you won't be upset if I disappear."

"Just find me by midnight. You know how I hate leaving those things alone—"

"Oh, I almost forgot. Elaine is hosting her first party without Steve."

"And?"

"And I promised her that you would make her a dress."

"Vinita, Steve left Elaine a wealthy woman. She can afford to buy a very nice dress."

"I know, but Elaine has no taste and she'll buy something awful again and everyone will talk about her behind her back. I couldn't take it, she's my best friend."

"Vinita—"

"And Olivia loves her."

"No."

"She's the best babysitter—"

"No."

"She never charges us."

"I don't have time."

"If you do this, I'll love you forever."

"Is that what it's going to take?"

She nodded.

After a pause, he said, "I'll make the dress."

Vinita smiled and leaned into Cruz for a kiss and he didn't notice, at that moment, the phone ringing or his children and Lourdes and Ana standing behind him watching him lean into an empty chair or Ivonne pick up the phone and say *the dress will be ready*. He didn't notice these things because he was too busy bringing the dinosaur back to life, feeding it satin, his foot dancing on the pedal as he chanted, *vada, arresto, vada, arresto* until the dress was finished and everyone was stunned by how flawless it was, the silhouette, the construction, the iridescent colors. Cruz handed the dress to Ivonne. She placed it on a hanger, picked up Vinita's jewelry box and headed to the garage. She heard Lourdes ask if she could handle it all on her own.

Ivonne turned and looked at everyone. She appeared frightened, exhausted. She walked up to Olivia and Luis, leaned in and whispered,

"Who wants to make a quarter?"

Later, in the backroom of a funeral home, Vinita lay on a table while a mortician watched her children fussing over their mother, adjusting this and that, the dress, the makeup, the hair, the jewelry, not leaving her side until everything was perfect.

# 38

At seventeen, after a story of mine won a writing contest, I told my mother I wanted to be a writer. She said we need to nurture this. When school ended that year, she sent me to Puerto Rico to live with my Grandmother Dolores for the summer so I could do nothing but write, instructing her mother not to assign me any chores or plan my days with outings, to set me up in her old room overlooking the coffee fields because her desk, all these years later, still looked brand new since she had rarely sat at it, unlike the worn and scratched desk that belonged to my Aunt Lourdes. On my first day there, my grandmother welcomed me with open arms, then I barely saw her again all summer except for occasional glimpses of her in the coffee fields or laughing on the porch with neighborhood women or driving off for the evening with a man. All my needs—my meals, my laundry—were taken care of by Gloria, the live-in housekeeper, the sweetest woman in the world. In the Bronx I would write in spurts whenever I found free time, blocking out the rest of the world, and by rest of the world, I mean the noise that was my brother and sister. It wasn't until that summer in Puerto Rico where I spent all day, every day, writing that I knew it was the only thing I wanted to do. I wasn't given any chores that summer though some nights I would help gather my grandmother's three dogs out of the coffee fields. If she was home, she'd call their names and they'd immediately come inside. On the nights she wasn't, Gloria and I would chase the dogs, sometimes for hours, herding them out of the coffee fields, leading them into the house with Gloria and I breathless and exhausted. But as exhausting as the dog herding was, it was still easier, much easier, than trying to herd my family now— scattered throughout my Los Angeles house— into a single room. They were in town for a dual celebration (my father's seventy-third birthday/the third anniversary of my mother's passing). They were all there. Papi, Ivonne, Luis, Aunt Lourdes, Ana. I could hear people everywhere. My assistant Mark by the pool on his telephone. Jane the housekeeper prepping lunch in the kitchen as she sang along to a song on the radio. Ivonne down the hall in the gym dropping weights. Luis chatting on his telephone in the dining room where a long table was set up for group meals that had not occurred because everyone ate at different times.

Upstairs I wandered the house comforting a trembling Cat in my arms, poor thing not used to so many people in the house. I turned a corner and ran into Papi, startling him and Cat who jumped out of my arms and ran off.

"Jesus, Olivia..." Papi placed a hand over his heart and took deep breaths.

"Sorry. Lunch is almost ready. I'm hoping we can all eat in the dining room."

"I'll eat in that room downstairs with the grey sofa. One of my shows is on."

"There are a few rooms with grey sofas."

"The one with the bookcases."

"The den."

"The den..." He looked around, confused.

"What do you need, Papi?"

"A map. Weren't there stairs here?"

"There are stairs that way that go to the main area, stairs back here that lead to the kitchen."

He sighed. As Papi walked away, he mumbled under his breath. "Awful lot of house for a woman and a cat."

Yesterday when we gathered around the kitchen island to sing "Happy Birthday" to Papi was the only time we've all been together. After he blew out the candles and the cake was eaten over small talk, everyone scattered like pigeons. To watch television, use the gym downstairs, make phone calls, drive to the ocean.

Everyone had arrived two days ago. They all seemed different here. On the rare occasions I spoke to the family, everyone's voice was always tinged with tension or anxiety or desperation, sometimes all three. Yet all that was gone once they arrived in California. Maybe it was the warmth and sunshine my mother always talked about that transformed everyone, including me, as soon as we stepped off the plane. Maybe it was natural mood stabilizers, grown locally, organically, scented with lavender then released into the California air. Issues that consumed our family when we did speak suddenly held no weight in California, quickly dismissed when they were brought up with a single word. *Whatever.*

Everyone arrived at different times. I had Mark pick them up at the airport though I made sure to greet them in my driveway when each one stepped out of the car. The solo arrivals allowed me to catch up with each one without being interrupted by another. I was so busy I rarely communicated with any of the family except for text messages here and there. I had no idea what was going on with anyone anymore. As soon as they stepped out of the car and the greetings and laughter ended, I demanded updates. My father had moved back to the Bronx a year ago. After one brutal winter, he returned to Phoenix recently, bought a small condo, said we could all visit anytime we want, there were plenty of nice hotels near him; Aunt Lourdes retired, downsized to a co-op apartment then quickly went back to teaching part time, confessing she spent a lot of time in classrooms long after her students had gone because that's the only place she's reminded of Javier anymore; Ana quit the diamond factory, got a job at a deaf school teaching sign language to children and her neighbors sit on her porch all the time and she asked me if I wanted Grandma's *Guernica* painting because it now lives in the back of a closet; Ivonne had told me two years ago that she bought her hair salon when she heard it was closing. Now she owns three salons in the Bronx where she sells a popular line of hair products she created and she's incorporated and thin and gorgeous and I hate her, I told her, and we laughed. Everyone was in a good place, in a good mood, and, again, I couldn't say if it was because we were in California or the fact that no one, including me, was tangled up in a complicated relationship.

Luis was the last to arrive. Scolding me for not returning his calls. Catching me up on the life of a busy medium. How he's booked a year in advance. How he can't believe he has people working for him. A booking manager, an assistant, an agent for TV appearances. He filled me in on life in the Bronx, the changes, the openings and closings of familiar places.

"Serrano's son is retiring, moving back to Puerto Rico and the family is selling the funeral home. I'm thinking of buying of it, maybe— god, I love this weather. I want to go out to Santa Monica Pier again—"

"Is she here?"

"What?"

"Mami. Is she here?"

"She's been here. Loves your new house, exactly what she always wanted for us. What's he doing...?" A gardener was watering plants. "Do your plants not like rainwater?"

"It hasn't rained in weeks."

"Then replace all this with rocks and desert stuff and stop wasting water."

"I like that idea. I'll have Mark look into it. C'mon." I took Luis' arm and we walked towards the house. "When's the last time you saw Ivonne?"

"Eight months, maybe longer. We're both so busy."

"Wait until you see how thin she is."

"She must've lined up her next husband."

"No, she didn't do it for some man. She says she has to maintain this image now for her salon customers—"

"Forget Ivonne. I want to know what's going on with *Northern U.* Tell me everything."

*Northern U* is a television drama I unintentionally pitched at a casual dinner with my agent and a producer who ended up selling it to a network. Unexpectedly I became a creator of this TV show that takes place at a university very much like the one I worked at. My goal was to illustrate the practical and emotional challenges of college life faced by faculty, staff, students. I wrote the first couple of episodes, pleased with the scripts, excited about the project. Then production began. The roles of the professors and students were cast with the most beautiful actors I had ever seen, looking like they spent more time at the gym than in a classroom. Rough cuts of the first two episodes were shown to network executives who sent back notes. One particular note caused me to lose all interest in the project: *More scenes in the bedroom.* I fought this until my agent asked me if I wanted to be labeled difficult so I complied. Filming wrapped, the show aired. Some critics were not kind but kinder than my own review. I waited for the show's quick cancellation which never came. We ended up being a ratings hit, less to do with my writing, more to do with viewers' interest in who was going to sleep with who. Though it has been financially lucrative for me, the show has not been a good experience, but my family is completely hooked on it which both amuses and annoys me. "The season finale shocked me," Luis said as we entered the house. "I can't wait until the fall, you have to tell me what happens." My family seemed pleased with my play when they saw it in New York, even enjoyed the film versions of my novels (except for Ivonne who—despite my denials that the novels were not about our family—was not pleased with the way our family was portrayed, she said, with the inaccuracies), but they enjoyed this TV show much, much more, sending me daily texts since the current season ended two months ago with a cliffhanger (a school shooting), grilling me for details, and when I wouldn't give them anything except explanations about how I'm just a producer now, how I don't write anything, I just review storylines and scripts they send me for approval, that arrive in emails I give as much interest to as I gave to the college papers I graded while I sat in the smallest office in the world way back when, more interested in the view outside my tiny window than the work in front of me.

Last week I realized I haven't done any of my own writing since those first episodes. I'm not a writer anymore. I'm a literary converter. I spend my days converting 300-page novels— written by others— into 120-page screenplays, feeling guilty for butchering another artist's work, something he or she spent years creating, then I come along with an ax, chopping away, saying we don't need that or that or that. The other day I complained to my agent about it. "This is temporary," he said, "until you're ready to write a story of your own. But until then, we have to keep the money coming in. We all have bills to take care of, mortgages to pay." I hung up the telephone and cried for two days. This wasn't the writer's life I had dreamed about when I was sitting by a window at my mother's old desk in Puerto Rico inhaling the smell of coffee all day.

By the end of my writing summer in Puerto Rico, Gloria had finally figured out the fastest way to get Grandmother's dogs out of the coffee fields and into the house. She would take leftovers from dinner, heat them in a large pot then place the steaming pot on the front porch, letting the aroma float out into the fields. Within minutes the dogs would start appearing one by one, following her into the house with pot in hand as I closed the door.

I passed by my home office. Ivonne was sitting at my desk on the telephone negotiating a deal, a salad in front of her. She acknowledged me with a nod and spun the swivel chair around until she faced the window. In the gym I found Luis exercising with the door open. He had his telephone on speaker, arguing with someone about his overbooked calendar. He waved at me, closed the door and carried on. I went into the empty dining room, the table still set up and untouched. I looked out a window. Aunt Lourdes and Ana were sitting at a table with sunglasses, signing to each other, drinks and food in front of them. Mark lay in a lounge chair at the other side of the pool texting on his telephone. I sent him a text. I watched him look at it and come inside. We walked in silence down a long hallway. Upon entering the screening room, Mark went up to the booth that held a movie projector and multiple media players that played DVDs, Blu-rays, VHS tapes. It was the reason why I bought the house, this screening room. It was the only house I saw where the screening room wasn't filled with oversized recliners that looked as if they could swallow you whole, more suitable for a nursing home than a screening room. This screening room felt like a real theatre with its vintage cinema seats covered in red velvet to match the red velvet drapes in front of the large screen which opened and closed at the push of a button. Off to the side, filled with various candies, was a vintage glass stand painted a deep red with three glass shelves resembling the concession stands in old movie lobbies my mother loved. To the right a striped, vintage popcorn maker filled with stale popcorn. Behind it, hidden in the wood-paneled wall, a refrigerator with all sorts of beverages, its door recessed in the wall and covered in wood to match the paneling. This was the second time the family had visited, and even though they had toured this room, no one had watched anything in here, choosing instead to go off on their own and sit in front of the various televisions scattered throughout the house.

I stood in front of the screen and sent a group text to the family:
*Surprise*
*they sent over rough cut of northern u season opener*
*come to the screening room*

Within minutes, the five of them, one by one, rushed into the screening room, more excited than my grandmother's dogs running out of the coffee field towards Gloria and her pot of leftovers. Some grabbed snacks or beverages. There were three rows of seats, yet everyone sat in the front row. Overlapping conversations occurred about the show, debates about who survived the school shooting, who didn't. Part of me wanted to laugh at them, the other part wanted to slap them.

I said, "While Mark gets things set up, I have an announcement."

The room fell silent. Everything I said from then on was accompanied by sign language.

"I'm going to Puerto Rico for a while."

"A vacation would do you good," someone said.

"I'm going there to write..."

My heart was racing. I could speak in front of studio executives and not break a sweat. But being around my family, let alone having to speak in front of them, has never been easy for me. Something about their kind of honesty has always caused me to go off to a corner and fade away.

My family was glancing at their watches or mobile phones. I took a deep breath. "I'm starting a new novel." Everyone looked up at me. "A memoir."

Ivonne opened her mouth, and before she could say anything, I said, "About Mami. Her time out here. Before you and Luis were born."

"So it'll be like your first two novels," Ivonne said, "except this time you're *not* going to change the names...Right?"

I prepared to argue then quickly surrendered. "Right."

A long silence.

Everyone stared at me as if they were trying to determine if I had anything else to say and if not, let's start the show. I looked up at Mark and saw he was still setting up so I continued to stall.

"I've been doing research," I said. "Trying to piece together Mami's life out here, the one she kept running back to..."

My family was feigning interest, looking up at Mark in the booth. Luis struggled to open a box of Raisinets, the plastic making all sorts of noise. Ivonne twisted open a Diet Coke that hissed at her.

"...I've been digging and found stuff like Mami's old apartment here, places she worked at and—with my connections at the studios—gained access to vaults, located one of Mami's actress friends out here though I haven't found her old agent J.J. a.k.a. Jeanine Jones. I started to wonder if she even existed—"

"Are we going to watch this show or not?"

I looked at everyone, feeling bad that I had herded them in there under false pretense. No one had sent anything over, there was no rough cut, no *Northern U* to show them. I looked up at the booth and Mark made a gesture at me. I moved and stood behind the glass stand.

The lights dimmed.

The room was silent, dark.

A black-and-white grainy screen.

The sound of static then silence.

A title screen appears...

From the front row, a collective gasp.
*On the screen, a handsome man in a suit and tie.*
*A knock on the door, he answers it.*
*Vinita stands there in a strapless evening gown.*
Another gasp from the front row.
*Her dress is dark to match her hair and eyes.*
*A woven bodice with a sweetheart neckline.*
*Cinched at her small waist then billows out.*
*A white pearl necklace, matching earrings.*
*Her hair a soft bob, her beauty undeniable.*
*She enters the room, looks around.*
I glanced at my family.
They looked like I did when I first saw it.
The mouth open, tears flowing.
*Vinita speaks naturally.*
*As if there were no camera there.*
*As if she'd been doing this all her life.*
*She and the man banter back and forth.*
*He wins her over, an embrace, a kiss.*
*She pulls away, starts to exit then turns back.*
*She says a line as the camera moves in.*
*She drops her purse, hesitates, looks at the ground.*
*She laughs, stops, then laughs some more.*

*Clearly this is not part of the scene.*
*She apologizes into the camera, picks up the purse.*
*Offscreen someone says* keep rolling.
*Then someone says a joke.*
*Mami laughs the way she used to when we were young.*
*She throws her head back having the time of her life.*
*In black and white for 149 seconds.*
*With no idea she'll spend years trying to get back here.*
*To this moment.*
*With a blue suitcase.*

# ABOUT RENÉ SOLIVAN

René Solivan's [December 15,1962 – July 13, 2023] fiction, poetry, drama and non-fiction have been published in magazines, literary journals and anthologies. Solivan is the winner of the Northridge Review Fiction Award, MetLife National Playwriting Award, and a Latino Theatre Initiative Emerging Artist Commission from the Mark Taper Forum (1977 Tony Award, Outstanding Regional Theatre) where Solivan was a playwriting fellow. The Taper produced a workshop of Solivan's play *Miss Lebron and Her Escorts* which was then developed at Off-Broadway's Obie award-winning Spanish Repertory Theatre starring NCIS star Cote de Pablo in the title role. René was nominated by Seattle Repertory Theatre (1990 Tony Award, Outstanding Regional Theatre) for the Mentor Project at the Cherry Lane Theatre in NYC. Solivan's play *Gods & Thieves* was presented at Geva Theatre; other plays have been seen on both coasts including his first play *Madre* which had its world premiere at Theatre/Theater in Hollywood where the *Los Angeles Times* hailed it as "an absorbing, compelling tour-de-force."

# ABOUT INLANDIA INSTITUTE

The Inlandia Institute is a regional literary non-profit and publishing house. We seek to bring focus to the richness of the literary enterprise that has existed in this region for ages.

The mission of Inlandia Books is to recognize, support, and expand literary activity in Inland Southern California by publishing works which deepen people's awareness, understanding, andappreciation of this unique, complex and creatively vibrant region. The mission is carried out by actively seeking out new works by writers who are affiliated with the region, and also through national literary competitions which elevate Inlandia Books to the national literary stage.

To learn more about the Inlandia Institute, please visit our website at www.InlandiaInstitute.org.

## INLANDIA BOOKS BY ELIUD MARTÍNEZ

*Güero-Güero: The White Mexican and Other Published and Unpublished Stories* by Dr. Eliud Martínez

## ELIUD MARTÍNEZ PRIZE SERIES

*Mexican Teeth: Stories and Assorted Artifacts of an Errant Chicanidad* by Tomás Hulick Baiza

*Search Party* by René Solivan

*Guajira, the Cuba girl* by Zita Arocha

## OTHER SELECTED INLANDIA BOOKS

*A Short Guide to Finding Your First Home in the United States: An Inlandia anthology on the immigrant experience*

*Apartness: A Memoir in Essays and Poems* by Judy Kronenfeld

*Breaking Pattern* by Tisha Marie Reichle-Aguilera

*Exit Prohibited* by Ellen Estilai

*Keep Sweet* by Victoria Waddle

*Razed: A Novel* by Thatcher Carter

*Scouts' Honor* by Carlos Cortés

*These Black Bodies Are...* edited by Romaine Washington

# ABOUT THE ELIUD MARTÍNEZ PRIZE

THE ELIUD MARTÍNEZ PRIZE was established to honor the memory of Eliud Martínez (1935–2020), artist, novelist, and professor emeritus of creative writing at the University of California, Riverside. One prize of $1,000 and book publication through Inlandia Books is awarded annually for a book of fiction or creative nonfiction by a writer who identifies as Hispanic, Latino/a/x, or Chicana/o/x.

*Our literary expression occupies a place within our American national literature, and among the literatures of the world.*

—Eliud Martinez